John Bunyan

A Book for Boys and Girls

Or, Country Rhymes for Childern

John Bunyan

A Book for Boys and Girls
Or, Country Rhymes for Childern

ISBN/EAN: 9783337138820

Printed in Europe, USA, Canada, Australia, Japan

Cover: Foto ©Andreas Hilbeck / pixelio.de

More available books at **www.hansebooks.com**

A

Book for Boys and Girls;

OR,

Country Rhymes for Children.

BY

JOHN BUNYAN.

BEING

*A FACSIMILE OF THE UNIQUE FIRST EDITION,
PUBLISHED IN 1686, DEPOSITED IN THE
BRITISH MUSEUM.*

WITH AN INTRODUCTION, GIVING AN ACCOUNT OF THE WORK,
BY REV. JOHN BROWN, D.D., AUTHOR OF "JOHN
BUNYAN : HIS LIFE, TIMES, AND WORK."

LONDON :
ELLIOT STOCK, 62, PATERNOSTER ROW.
1889.

INTRODUCTION.

WHEN Mr. Offor published his complete edition of Bunyan's Works in 1862, he, of course, included in the collection the little book issued in Bunyan's name, and long known under the title of "Divine Emblems." At the same time he said in the preface that a mystery hung over this little work which many years' diligent research had not enabled him to solve. For in the two lists of Bunyan's Works made by Charles Doe in 1692 and 1698, there is no mention made of any book bearing the title referred to, nor is there any such title to be found in the many advertisements of his works issued by Bunyan's own publishers. Some clue to the mystery seemed to be offered in the fact that a work with a different title, but identical with the " Divine Emblems" in other respects, was published in 1701 as "A Book for Boys and Girls; or, Temporal Things Spiritualized," by John Bunyan. The natural conclusion was that this was the same work as the one numbered thirty-seven in Charles Doe's list of 1698, and described as " A Book for Boys and Girls; or, Country Rhymes for Children in Verse on `Seventy-four Things;" and, in the list of 1692, as "Meditations on Seventy - four Things." Under one or other of these two titles also the book was advertised as Bunyan's, both by Nathaniel Ponder and Dorman Newman—the one the publisher of the " Pilgrim's Progress," and the other of the " Holy War." That Bunyan had published some book of the kind there could therefore be no doubt, but here came the difficulty: the " Divine Emblems" contained only forty-nine similes, whereas, as we have seen, the original work was described as "Meditations on Seventy-four Things." How did the seventy-four turn out to be only forty-nine? Mr. Offor made the ingenious suggestion that in the later work two emblems had in some instances been run together into one. For example, the first emblem in the later edition contains meditations on two things — the Barren Fig-tree and God's Vineyard ; and the second has a meditation on the Lark and the Fowler, and also a comparison between the Fowler and Satan. It may be, Mr. Offor suggested, that these two emblems were in this way originally four, and so with others ; and upon this plan the volume contained exactly seventy-four meditations.

This was ingenious, but not satisfactory ; and the real truth could only be arrived at when a copy of the original work, as Bunyan sent it forth in 1686, should happen to turn up. There seemed but faint hope of this, however, for though the book has gone through many editions, it has, ever since 1701, been published only in the shortened form in which we have been so long familiar with it ; all through the eighteenth century, therefore, no copy of the original seems to have been within reach of any of the publishers. Moreover Mr. Offor, one of the most indefatigable of collectors, had, as he tells us, made most diligent inquiry for this first edition both in the United Kingdom and in America, but all in vain.

And now, thirty years after his long and fruitless search, when no one was thinking very much about the missing book, it has, within the last few months, unexpectedly turned up, and is here presented to the reader in *facsimile*. Its history, so far as we can arrive thereat, is curious and interesting. It appears originally to have belonged to the well-known seventeenth-century diarist, Narcissus Luttrell, who bought it for sixpence, the price at which it was first issued, on May 12, 1686. In the Luttrell Collection, now in the British Museum, there is a broadside of Bunyan's entitled "A Caution to Stir up to Watch against Sin." On this sheet Narcissus Luttrell has written the price, one penny, and the date of purchase, "8 Aprill, 1684." In like manner, on the title-page of this newly-acquired copy of "A Book for Boys and Girls," there is recorded the price and date of purchase, the record both on broadside and title-page being evidently in the same handwriting, the style being the same, and a marked peculiarity about the letter "d" occurring in both cases. The broadside in question seems to have passed from its first purchaser, Luttrell, to the Duke of Buckingham, forming part of the Stowe Collection, and it is not improbable that the book before us went with it at the same time to the same destination. Here in the dignified repose common to ducal libraries, these "Country Rhymes" probably remained undisturbed all through the eighteenth century, and on into the nineteenth; and on the breaking up of the great collection of which it formed part, it seems to have found its way back again into the hands of the trade. What happened to it in the interval we have no means of knowing; all that we do know with certainty is that some six or seven years ago it was purchased for forty guineas from a London bookseller by a gentleman from New York, and that a few months ago this gentleman sold part of his valuable collection, which was purchased by Mr. Henry N. Stevens, of Great

Russell Street, among the books thus sold
being the one before us. It was shortly
after acquired by the authorities of the
British Museum ; and thus, after being in
two well-known collections, yet dropping
out of public knowledge for more than
a century and a half, twice crossing the
Atlantic and now coming once more to the
light, this little work from the pen of the
Dreamer has at length found a final resting-
place in the great library of the nation.

Looking at the work as we have it now
in its complete form, we find that Mr.
Offor's suggestion was not the true ex-
planation. There was no running of two
similes into one, but the original seventy-
four meditations were reduced, in 1701, to
forty-nine by simply dropping twenty-five
out of the book altogether. Those left
out were the Meditations numbered I., II.,
X., XXIV., XXVII., XXVIII., XXIX.,
XL., XLVII., XLIX., LI., LIV., LV.,
LVI., LX., LXII., LXIII., LXIV., LXV.,
LXVII., LXVIII., LXIX., LXXI.,
LXXII., LXXIV. Other changes also
were introduced. The curious little sub-
stitute for a horn-book at the beginning,

entitled "An Help to Children to learn
to read English," was taken away, and,
consequent upon this, the last twelve lines
of the poetical address to the reader also.
It is somewhat difficult for us to imagine
Bunyan writing out half a dozen different
alphabets, giving lists of vowels and con-
sonants, and teaching children to spell the
simple words of their own tongue, or to
spell aright their own Christian names.
Yet here we have the thing before us.
It may be that our old friend Nathaniel
Ponder, the publisher, made this addition
himself by way of meeting the wants of
the boys and girls, for whom the book
was intended, in days when spelling-books
were not so plentiful as they have sinc
become. Still, in the closing lines of the
address to the reader, as it originally stood,
Bunyan claims this work as his own, and
the last three in the list of names of girls
—Christiana, Katherine, Frances—are dis-
tinctly Bunyanish, the first being the name
of his own heroine, and the other two
names in his own family. Probably, by
way of making up for the removal of so
much matter from the beginning and the

body of the work, there was added to it at the end the poem by Bunyan, originally sold as a broadside, and entitled " A Caution to Stir Up to Watch against Sin."

While several of the meditations were taken away entirely, many of those remaining were subjected to considerable revision. The unknown editor of 1701 set about doing for these " Country Rhymes " what Joshua Gilpin, the pious but mistaken Vicar of Wrockwardine, attempted some eighty years ago to do for Bunyan's greater work, the " Pilgrim's Progress." To this worthy vicar it seemed desirable that " the excellent, though illiterate, Bunyan should be made to speak with a little more grammatical precision ; that his extreme coarseness should be moderately abated ; that he should be rendered less obscure in some passages, less tautological in others, and offensive in none." This attempt to translate Bunyan's racy English into high-sounding Johnsonese ended, as might be expected, in producing a book which no one cared to read, and the popular instinct, sounder than the pedantic, prefers Bunyan in his seventeenth - century doublet to Bunyan in eighteenth-century buckram.

Exception may be taken in the same way, though not to the same extent, to the revision of this " Book for Boys and Girls," which took place in 1701. The reader, glancing over two or three of the meditations left out, may be inclined to think that a little of their seventeenth-century naturalism might very well be spared ; at the same time, while some changes were perhaps necessary, the changes made were not in every case improvements. For example, Bunyan, speaking of some who think much of the decoration of their houses, and the adornment of their persons, says :

" Meanwhile their soul lies ley has no good in 't."

This expression, " lies ley," which, of course, means to lie fallow, uncultivated, the editor tames down into :

"While their immortal soul has no good in 't."

" Pretty taking notes" is weakened into " pretty tuneful notes." In its original form, the meditation on the rising of the sun is put thus :

> " The night is gone, the shadows fled away,
> And we now most sure are that it is day ;
> Our Eyes behold, and our Hearts believe it,
> Nor can the wit of man in this deceive it."

This is shortened to :

> " The night is gone, the shadows fled away,
> And now we are most certain that 'tis day."

The boy spoken of in the forty-sixth meditation was reminded that he must be careful with his watch, and wind it duly :

> " Or else your watch, were it as good again,
> Would not with time and tide you entertain."

This was put more baldly thus :

> " Or else your watch will not exactly go—
> 'Twill stand or run too fast, or move too slow."

There are those, Bunyan tells us in the fifty-ninth simile, who give no response even to skilfullest music, and like to these are those who lie

> " Under the Word, without the least advance
> Godward : such do despise the Ministry."

This is spoilt, rather than improved, by
being put into this shape :

" They lie
Under the Word, without the least advance :
Such do despise the Gospel Ministry."

Passing by these, and other illustrations
of doubtful editing, and coming to the
book itself, we are impressed anew with the
fact that Bunyan was an allegorist, rather
than a poet. Yet a poet he aspired to be.
" Man's heart is apt in metre to delight,"
says he in one place, and he indulged himself in this direction to an extent which
is not always realized. If all his poetical
efforts were brought together, they would,
in point of bulk, make a considerable
volume. In the very first year of his long
imprisonment, he solaced the tedium of
Bedford Gaol by sending forth his " Profit-
able Meditations," a work in nine sections,
and running into a hundred and eighty-
six stanzas. Three years later, in 1664,
while still a prisoner, he published his
poetical " Meditations on the Four Last
Things," to which he added, " Ebal and
Gerizzim ; or, The Blessing and the
Curse," the former extending to about

twelve hundred lines, and the latter to eight hundred. A year later he sent forth his " Prison Meditations " in seventy stanzas, in which occur the well-known lines :

> " For though men keep my outward man
> Within their locks and bars,
> Yet by the faith of Christ I can
> Mount higher than the stars."

There are weighty reasons for not accepting the work known as " Scriptural Poems," and usually attributed to Bunyan, as genuine. But passing by these, for something like twenty years after the appearance of his early prison books, his only attempts in the direction of poetry were confined to seven stanzas inserted in the work known as " The Greatness of the Soul "; the broadside issued in 1684, entitled " A Caution to Stir Up to Watch against Sin "; the poetical introductions to the first and second parts of the " Pilgrim's Progress," and to the " Holy War," and the verses inserted here and there in the " Pilgrim," and including the Shepherd Boy's Song, and the charming lyric beginning,

" Who would true valour see
    Let him come hither ;
  One here will constant be,
    Come wind, come weather."

In the last year of his life, 1688, Bunyan sent forth what in point of length may be regarded as his most considerable poetical venture, the work entitled " A Discourse of the Building, Nature, Excellency, and Government of the House of God." This extended to nearly fourteen hundred lines, and is a kind of development of the idea of the Palace Beautiful of his Pilgrim story.

The " Book for Boys and Girls " now before us preceded this later work by about two years, being published in 1686. In a characteristic preface he tells his readers that this little book of his is meant for boys and girls, slyly adding that he means those of all ages and of all sorts and degrees ; for often our bearded men do act like beardless boys ; our women please themselves with childish toys. To do good to these juveniles of all ages, he will come down to meet them :

" Good reader that I save them may,
I now with them the very Dotteril play.

And since at Gravity they make a Tush,
My very Beard I cast behind the Bush.
And like a Fool stand fing'ring of their Toys ;
And all to show them they are Girls and Boys."

He could, he says, were he so pleased, use higher strains, but what would be the practical good of that ? The arrow gone out of sight awakes not the sleeper. To shoot too high may set mere children on the upward gaze ; but it is that which hits a man doth him amaze. Paul played the fool sometimes, that he might the better catch those that were fools indeed ; and he himself will not hesitate to follow so good an example.

In some of these meditations he recurs to similes he has already set forth in earlier works. The thirty-third, for example, "The Barren Fig-tree," was the subject of one of his most searching treatises, published some four years earlier, and in which he had shown that the cumber-ground must to the wood-pile, and thence to the fire. The longest in the series, that on "The Sinner and the Spider," had more than once occupied his thoughts before. In a book of his published in 1675, and entitled "Light for Them that

Sit in Darkness," he shows that the soul in temptation is like a fly in a spider's web : " The fly is entangled in the web ; at this the spider shows himself; if the fly stir again, down comes the spider to her and claps a foot upon her ; if yet the fly makes a noise, then with poisoned mouth the spider lays hold upon her ; if the fly struggle still, then he poisons her more and more. What shall the fly do now ?" In the second part of his " Pilgrim " also the same illustration, with a different application, comes back to him, when Interpreter shows Christiana and her companions a very great spider on the wall, and they have edifying discourse thereupon.

Passing to some of the other meditations contained in the book, we feel how aptly Bunyan has been described as a religious Æsop, with a fable for everything. His imagination was ever with him the dominant faculty, and here, as elsewhere in his works, it plays with all sorts of fancies, but always with serious purpose. Great truths are shown to be nestling for us under leaves of simplest circumstance—

> " The swan on still Saint Mary's lake,
> Floats double, Swan and Shadow."

Similes are seen everywhere. The sky with its ever-varying phenomena ; human life with its frailties and pathos, its follies and sublimities ; the birds and beasts with their suggestive relations to each other and to man ; natural objects, with their power of throwing light upon the supernatural ; all come and go in these pages, leaving lessons to make us wiser. Alexander Smith, the Glasgow poet, said of the book : " Bunyan's muse is clad in russet, wears shoes and stockings, has a country accent, and walks along the level Bedfordshire roads. But if as a poet he is homely and idiomatic, he is always natural, straightforward, and sincere. His lines are unpolished, but they have pith and sinew, like the talk of a shrewd peasant. There are here also many touches of pure poetry, showing that in his mind there was a vein of silver which, under favourable circumstances, might have been worked to rich issues ; and everywhere there is an admirable homely pregnancy and fulness of meaning."

In the complete book, as we now have it, there are one or two additional meditations which have a sort of autobiographic interest. The child awakened from his dream (No. II.) utters this lamentation :

> " I have in sin abounded,
> My heart therewith is wounded,
> With fears I am surrounded,
> My Spirit is confounded."

We recall, as we read this, that Bunyan tells us how, because of his sins, "the Lord, even in my childhood, did scare and affright me with fearful dreams, and did terrify me with dreadful visions." The meditation upon a ring of bells (No. XXIX.) also seems to take us back to Elstow steeple and the old days when he so dearly loved to join the ringers. The comparisons are vivid throughout. His body is the steeple, where the bells, the powers of his soul, do hang ; the clappers are the passions of his mind ; while the ropes are the promises, and God-given graces the ringers :

> " Let not my Bells these Ringers want, nor Ropes ;
> Yea, let them have room for to swing and sway."

He had seen village lads steal into Elstow
steeple, and make jangle with the bells ; so
did the lusts of his body sometimes into
the belfry go :

"Then, Lord, I pray thee keep my Belfry Key,
    Let none but Graces meddle with these Ropes."

We have now also, for the first time,
curiously enough, staves of music given to
which two of the Meditations (XXXI. and
XXXIV.) were evidently to be sung. The
clef in both cases is obsolete now, being
printed in the shape in which it is found in
Christopher Simpson's " Compendium of
Practical Musick," 1678. This is a sort of
middle term between the form given in
1653, by Henry Lawes, in his " Ayres and
Dialogues for one, two, and three voyces,"
and that found in Playford's Psalms of
1697. The printing of this music, as will
be seen, is rather rudely executed, and in
the first of the two melodies given there
appear to be two notes left out. We have
also for the first time in this edition a
rhyming version of the Apostles' Creed
(No. X.), possibly another reminiscence
of Elstow Church and his earlier days.
    The rest of the twenty-five meditations

now restored to us have very much the same character as those with which we have been long familiar. The fatted swine being made ready for the butcher's stall reminds him of the gross overfed men of the world ripening for judgement; the postboy hurrying along and allowing none to give him stop or stay is suggestive of the zeal of the true pilgrim on his way heavenward; the boy with his paper of plums, which he counts so much better than bread, like Passion in the "Pilgrim," soon spends his delights and comes back by-and-by with nought but paper and thread; the brave weathercock faces the wind, blow from what quarter it may, so should the Christian face Antichrist in each disguise; finally, the horse that starts and snorts at sound of drum is like those Christian professors who cannot face trials and persecutions for their faith. Others there are of firmer soul, of whom Bunyan himself was one, who from the drum will neither start nor flee,

"Let Drummers beat the charge or what they will,
They'll nose them, face them, keep their places still."

We may now close this foreword with
a brief reference to some of the editions
through which this book has passed since
its first appearance. Published in 1686, it
was never reprinted in Bunyan's lifetime.
In 1701 it reappeared with all the changes
to which reference has been made. The
title-page then ran as follows: "A Book
for Boys and Girls; or, Temporal Things
Spiritualized. By John Bunyan. Licensed
and entered according to Order. London :
Printed for, and sold by, R. Tookey, at
his Printing House, in St. Christopher's
Court, in Threadneedle Street, behind the
Royal Exchange, 1701." Of this second
edition the only known copy existing is
in the Bodleian Library. There were no
illustrations to the book till 1707, when
the third edition appeared, which, according to an advertisement of the period, was
"ornamented with cuts." The earliest
copy now in existence, next to the second,
is one of the ninth edition, which appeared
in 1724, and bore, for the first time, the
title which the book has ever since re-
tained : "Divine Emblems ; or, Temporal
Things Spiritualized." This was "adorned

with cuts suitable to every subject." Suitable they might be, but fearsome to see
they certainly were. In 1757 a tenth
edition was published by E. Dilly, at the
Rose and Crown, in the Poultry. This
was embellished with a new set of engravings, executed in better style. The
costumes depicted, as might be expected,
were those of the early Georgian period,
the ladies standing out with hooped
petticoats and high head-dresses, and the
men with cocked hats and queues. These
engravings were again and again repeated,
and were reproduced in good style a few
years ago by Bickers and Son, in an
edition containing a preface by Alexander
Smith. This edition of 1757 had a curious
preface signed " J. D.," and " addressed to
the Great Boys in Folio and the Little
Ones in Coats." What this preface had
to do with the book it is somewhat difficult to see, inasmuch as it is mainly con-
cerned with showing " that Language came
originally by Revelation of God, and not
by Chance, nor invented by Artifice."
About 1790 a very pretty edition of the
" Divine Emblems" was issued, " En-

graved, printed, and sold by T. Bennett,
of Plough Court, Fetter Lane." It was
in square 16mo., and was remarkable not
merely for the excellence of its illustrations, but also for the unusual circumstance
that not merely these, but the entire book,
from the title-page to the end, was en-
graved and printed from copper plates.
The only known copy of this edition is
now before the present writer, having been
saved from the ruin of Mr. Offor's collection, the pages being complete, but the
back and binding entirely burnt away.
A handsome edition, with superior illustrations, was also edited by W. Mason,
and published by Alexander Hogg, in
1780. Other editions were issued in
London in 1790 and 1793 by C. Dilly, and
in 1802 by J. Mawman, in the Poultry ;
and in Coventry by M. Luckman (N. D.)
and N. Merridew, 1806, but they do not
call for special remark.

A
BOOK
FOR
BOYS
AND
GIRLS:
OR,
Country Rhimes
FOR
Children.

By *J. B.*

Licenſed and Entred according to Order.

LONDON, Printed for *N. P.* and Sold by the Bookſellers in *London* 1686.

TO THE
READER

Courteous Reader,

The Title-page will shew, if there thou look,
  Who are the proper Subjects of this Book.
They'r Boys and Girls of all Sorts and Degrees,
From those of Age, to Children on the Knees.
Thus comprehensive am I in my Notions;
They tempt me to it by their childish Motions.
We now have Boys with Beards, and Girls that be
Big as old Women, wanting Gravity.

Then do not blame me, 'cause I thus describe them;
Flatter I may not, lest thereby I bribe them
To have a better Judgment of themselves,
Than wise men have of Babies on their Shelves.
Their antick Tricks, fantastick Modes, and way,
Shew they like very Boys, and Girls, do play
With all the frantick Fopp'ries of this Age;
And that in open view, as on a Stage;
Our Bearded men, do act like Beardless Boys;
Our Women please themselves with childish Toys.

Our Ministers, long time by Word and Pen,
Dealt with them, counting them, not Boys but Men:
Thunder-bolts they shot at them, and their Toys:
But hit them not, 'cause they were Girls and Boys.

The better Charge, the wider still they shot,
Or else so high, these Dwarfs they touched not.
Instead of Men, they found them Girls and Boys,
Addict to nothing as to childish Toys.

Wherefore good Reader, that I save them may,
I now with them, the very Dottril play.
And since as Gravity they make a Tush,
My very Beard I cast behind the Bush.
And like a Fool stand fing'ring of their Toys ;
And all to shew them, they are Girls and Boys.

Nor do I blush, although I think some may
Call me a Baby, 'cause I with them play :
I do't to shew them how each Fingle-fangle,
On which they doting are, their Souls entangle,
As with a Web, a Trap, a Ginn, or Snare .
And will destroy them, have they not a Care,

Paul seem'd to play the Fool, that he might gain
Those that were Fools indeed, if not in Grain.
And did it by their things, that they might know
Their emptiness, and might be brought unto
What would them save from Sin and Vanity.
A Noble Act, and full of Honesty.

Yet he, nor I would like them be in Vice,
While by their Play-things, I would them entice,
To mount their Thoughts from what are childish Toys,
To Heav'n, for that's prepar'd for Girls and Boys.
Nor do I so confine my self to these,
As to shun graver things, I seek to please,
Those more compos'd with better things than Toys:
Tho thus I would be catching Girls and Boys.

Wherefore

Wherefore if Men have now a mind to look ;
Perhaps their Graver Fancies may be took
With what is here ; tho but in Homely Rhimes :
But he, who pleases all, must rise betimes.
Some, I perswade me, will be finding Fault,
Concluding, here I trip, and there I halt,
No doubt some could these groveling Notions raise
By fine-spun Terms that challenge might the Bays.
But should all men be fore't to lay aside
Their Brains, that cannot regulate the Tide
By this or that man's Fancy, we should have
The Wise, unto the Fool, become a Slave
What tho my Text seems mean, my Morals be
Grave, as if fetch't from a Sublimer Tree.
And if some better handle can a Fly,
Then some a Text, why should we them deny
Their making Proof, or good Experiment,
Of smallest things great mischiefs to prevent ?
   Wise Solomon did Fools to Pismants send,
To learn true Wisdom, and their Lives to mend.
Yea, God by Swallows, Cuckows, and the Ass ;
Shews they are Fools who let that season pass,
Which he put in their hand, that to obtain
Which is both present, and Eternal Gain.
   I think the wiser sort my Rhimes may slight
But what care I ! The foolish will delight
To read them. and the Foolish, God has chose.
And doth by Foolish Things, thew minds compose,
And settle upon that which is Divine :
Great Things, by little ones, are made to shine.

I could, were I so pleas'd, use higher Strains.
And for Applause, on Tenters stretch my Brains,
But what needs that? The Arrow out of Sight,
Does not the Sleeper, nor the Watchman fright.
To shoot too high doth but make Children gaze,
Tis that which hits the man, doth him amaze.
　　And for the Inconsiderableness
Of things, by which I do my mind express;
May I by them bring some good thing to pass,
As Sampson, with the Jaw-bone of an Ass;
Or as Brave Shamgar with his Oxe's Goad,
(Both things not manly, nor for War in Mode
I have my end, tho I my self expose
To scorn; God will have Glory in the close.
　　Thus much for artificial Babes; and now
To those who are in years but such, I bow
　　My Pen to teach them what the Letters be,
And how they may improve their A, B, C.
Nor let my pretty Children them despise;
All, needs must there begin, that wou'd be wise
　　Nor let them fall under Discouragement,
Who at their Horn-book stick, and time hath spent
Upon that A, B, C. while others do
Into their Primer, or their Psalter go.
Some Boys with difficulty do begin,
Who in the end, the Bays, and Laurel win.

J. B.

An

In or-der to the at-tain-ing of which, they must first be taught the Let-ters, which be these that fol low,

𝕬 𝕭 𝕮 𝕯 𝕰 𝕱 𝕲 𝕳 𝕴 𝕶 𝕷 𝕸 𝕹 𝕺 𝕻 𝕼 𝕽 𝕾 𝕿 𝖀 𝖂.

a b c d e f g h i k l m n o p q r ſ t u w x y z.
A B C D E F G H I K L M N O P Q R S T V W
X Y Z.

a b c d e f g h i k l m n o p q r ſ t v u w x y z
ABCDEFGHIKLMNOPQRSTVW
XTZ

a b c d e f g h i k l m n o p q r ſ t v u w x y z
The Vowels are these, a, e, i, o, u.

As there are vow-els, ſo are there Con-ſo-nants, and they are theſe.

b c d f g h k l m n p q r ſ t v w x y z.
There are alſo dou-ble Let-ters, and they are theſe.

ct ſſ ſi ſſi fl fi ffi ſt ſh.

Af-ter theſe are known, then ſet your Child to ſpel-ling, Thus T-o, to. T-h-e, the, O-r, or, I f, if I-n, in, M e, me, y-o-u, you; f-i-n-d, find, S-i-n, ſin: In C-h-ri-ſ-t, Chriſt, i-s, is, R-i-g-h-t-e-o u-ſ-n e-ſs, Righ-te-ouſ-neſs.

And ob-ſerve that e-ve-ry word or ſyl-la-ble (tho ne-ver ſo ſmall) muſt have one vow-el or more right-ly pla-ced in it.

For inſtances, Theſe are no words nor Syl-la-bles, be-cauſe they have no vow-els in them, name-ly, fl, gld, ſtrnght, ſpll, drll, fll.

Words made of two Letters are theſe, and ſuch-like, If, it, us, ſo, do, we, ſee, he, is, in, my.

Words con-ſiſt-ing of three Letters,

But, for, her, ſhe, did, doe, all, his, way, you, may, ſay, nay.

Names

To learn Chil-dren to spell a-right their names.

Names of Boys.	Names of Girls.
Tho-mas.	An-na.
James.	Su-san-na.
S-mon.	Re-be-kah.
Ed-ward.	Mag-da-lene.
John.	E-li-za-beth.
Ro-bert.	Sa-rah.
Richard.	Ma-ry.
Ad-am	Jane.
Ti-mo-thy.	Dor-cas.
Ja-cob.	Ra-chel.
A-bra-ham	Di-nah.
Mo-ses	Do-ro-thy.
Aa-ron,	Joanna.
Phi-lip.	Ly-di-a.
Mat-thew.	Da-ma-ris.
Bar-tho-lo-mew	A-bi-gail.
Wil-li-am.	Mi-chal.
Hen-ry	Han-nah.
Ralph.	Ruth.
Ste-phen.	Mar-tha.
Je-re-mi-ah	Ag-nis.
Pe-ter.	Mar-ga-ret,
George	Ju-dith.
Jo-nas.	Joan.
A-mos.	Alice.
Ni-cho-las	Phe-be.
Job	Grace.
Da-vid.	Chris-ti-a-na.
	Ka-the-rine.
	Fran-ces.

To ,

Figures.	Numeral Letters
1. One.	I. One.
2. Two.	I L Two.
3. Three.	I I L Three.
4. Four.	I V. Four.
5. Five.	V. Five.
6. Six.	V I Six.
7. Seven.	V I I. Seven.
8. Eight.	V I I I. Eight.
9. Nine.	I X. Nine.
10. Ten.	X. Ten.
11. Eleven.	X I. Eleven.
12. Twelve.	X I I. Twelve.
13. Thirteen.	X I I I. Thirteen.
14. Fourteen.	X I V. Fourteen.
15. Fifteen.	X V. Fifteen.
16. Sixteen.	X V I Sixteen.
17. Seventeen.	X V I I. Seventeen.
18. Eighteen.	X V I I I. Eighteen.
19. Nineteen.	X I X. Nineteen.
20. Twenty.	X X. Twenty.
30. Thirty.	X X X. Thirty.
40. Forty.	X L. Forty.
50. Fifty.	L. Fifty.
60. Sixty.	L X. Sixty.
70. Seventy.	L X X. Seventy.
80. Eighty.	L X X X. Eighty.
90. Ninety.	X C. Ninety.
100. a Hundred.	C. a Hundred.
500. Five hundred.	D. Five hundred.
1000. a Thousand.	M. a Thousand.

I shall forbear to add more, being perswaded this is enough for little Children to prepare themselves for Psalter, or Bible.

A

A BOOK

FOR

Boys and Girls, &c.

I.

Upon the Ten Commandments.

1. THou fhalt not have another God than me :.
2. Thou fhalt not to an Image bow thy Knee.
3. Thou fhalt not take the Name of God in vain :
4. See that the Sabbath thou do not profain .
5. Honour thy Father and thy Mother to :
6. In Act or Thought fee thou no Murder do.
7. From Fornication keep thy body clean :
8. Thou fhalt not fteal, though thou be very mean.
6. Bear no falfe Witnefs, keep thee without Spot:
10. What is thy Neighbours fee thou Covet not.

B   II

II

The awakened Childs Lamentation.

VVHen *Adam* was deceived,
    I was of Life bereaved ;
Of late (too) I perceived,
I was in ſin conceived.

2.

And as I was born naked,.
I was with filth beſpaked,
At which when I awaked,
My Soul and Spirit ſhaked.

3.

My Filth grew ſtrong, and boyled,
And me throughout defiled,
Its pleaſures me beguiled,
My Soul ! how art thou ſpoyled !

My Joys with ſinwere painted,
My mind with ſin is tainted,
My heart with Guilt is fainted,
I wa'nt with God acquainted.

5.

I have in ſin abounded,
My heart therewith is wounded,

With

with fears I am furrounded,
My Spirit is confounded.

6.

I have been often called,
By fin as oft enthralled,
Pleafures hath me fore-ftalled.
How is my Spirit gauled !

7.

As fin has me infected,
I am thereof detected :
Mercy I have neglected,
I fear I am rejected.

8.

The Word I have mif-ufed
Good Council too refufed ;
Thus I my Self abufed ;
How can I be excufed?

9.

When other Children prayed,
That work I then delayed,
Ran up and down and played ,
And thus from God have ftrayed.

10.

Had I in God delighted,
And my wrong doings righted ;
I had not thus been frighted,
Nor as I am benighted.

11.

O! That God would be pleafed,
T'wards me to be appeafed ;

And

And heal me thus diſeaſed,
How ſhould I then be eaſed !

12.

But Truth I have deſpiſed,
My follies idolized,
Saints with Reproach diſguiſed,
Salvation nothing prized.

13.

O Lord! I am aſhamed ,
When I do hear thee named ;
'Cauſe thee I have defamed,
And liv'd like Beaſts untamed !

14.

Would God I might be ſaved,
Might have an heart like *David* ;
This I have ſometimes craved,
Yet am by ſin enſlaved !

15.

Vanity I have loved,
My heart from God removed ;
And not, as me behoved,
The means of Grace improved.

16.

O Lord! if I had cryed
(When I told tales and lyed)
For Mercy, and denyed
My Luſts, I had not died !

17.

But Mercies-Gate is locked,
Yea, up that way is blocked;

Yea fome that there have knocked,
God at their cryes hath mocked.

18.

'Caufe him they had difdained,
Their wicked ways maintained,
From Godlinefs refrained,
And on his word complained.

19.

I would I were converted
Would fin and I were parted,
For folly I have fmarted;
God make me honeft-hearted!

20.

I have to Grace appealed,
Would 'twere to me revealed,
And Pardon to me fealed,
Then fhould I foon be healed!

21

Whofe Nature God hath mended,
Whofe finful courfe is ended,
Who is to life afcended,
Of God is much befriended.

22.

Oh! Were I reconciled
To God, I, tho defiled,
Should be as one that fmiled,
To think my death was fpoiled.

23.

Lord; thou waft crucified
For Sinners, bled and dyed,.

I have for Mercy cryed,
Let me not be denyed.

24
I have thy Spirit grieved;
Yet is my life reprieved,
Would I in thee believed,
Then I should be·relieved.

25.
Were but Repentance gained,
And had I Faith unfeigned,
Then Joy would be maintained
In me, and sin restrained.

26.
But this is to be noted,
I have on Folly doted,
My Vanities promoted,
My self to them devoted.

27.
Thus I have sin committed,
And so my self out-witted;
Yea, and my Soul unfitted,
To be to Heaven admitted.

28.
But God has condescended,
And pardon has extended,
To such as have offended,
Before their lives were ended.

29.
O Lord! do not disdain me,
But kindly entertain me;

Yea in thy Faith maintain me,
And let thy Love conftrain me!

III

Meditations upon an Egg.

1

THe Egg's no Chick by falling from the Hen;
Nor man a Chriftian, till he's born agen.
The Egg's at firft contained in the Shell;
Men afore Grace, in fins, and darknefs dwell.
The Egg when laid,by Warmth is made a Chicken;
And Chrift, by Grace, thofe dead in fin doth quicken.
The Egg, when firft a Chick,the fhell's its Prifon;
So's flefh to th'Soul, who yet with Chrift is rifen.
The Shell doth crack, the Chick doth chirp and
The flefh decays, as men do pray and weep. (peep;
The Shell doth break, the Chick's at liberty;
The flefh falls off, the Soul mounts up on high.
But both do not enjoy the felf-fame plight;
The Soul is fafe, the Chick now fears the Kite.

2.

But Chick's from rotten Eggs do not proceed;
Nor is an Hypocrite a Saint indeed.
The rotten Egg, though underneath the Hen,
If crack'd, ftinks, and is loathfome unto men.
Nor doth her Warmth make what is rotten found,
What's rotten, rotten will at laft be found.

The

The Hyppocrite, fin has him in Poffeffion,
He is a rotten Egg under Profeffion.

3.

Some Eggs bring Cockatrices; and fome men
Seem hatcht and brooded in the Vipers Den.
Some Eggs bring wild-Fowls;and fome men there be
As wild as are the wildeft Fowls that flee.
Some Eggs bring Spiders; and fome men appear
More venom than the worft of Spiders are.
Some Eggs bring Pifs ants; and fome feem to me
As much for trifles as the Pifs-ants be.
Thus divers Eggs do produce divers fhapes,
As like fome Men as Monkeys are like Apes.
But this is but an Egg, were it a Chick,
Here had been Legs, and Wings, and Bones to pick.

I V.

Upon the Lord's Prayer.

OUr Father which in Heaven art;
   Thy name be always hallowed;
Thy Kingdom come, thy Will be done;
Thy Heav'nly path be followed.
  By us on Earth as 'tis with thee,
  We humbly pray;
  And let our Bread us given be
  From day to day.
  Forgive our debts, as we forgive
Thofe that to us indebted are:

ıto temptation lead us not ;
ıut fave us from the wicked's Snare.
  The Kingdom's thine, the Power too,
  we thee adore ,
  The Glory alfo fhall be thine
  For evermore.

V

Meditation upon Peep of day.

I Oft, though it be peep of day, do'nt know,
  Whether 'tis Night, whether 'tis Day or no.
I fancy that I fee a little light ;
But cannot yet diftinguifh day from night.
I hope, I doubt, but fteddy yet I be not,
I am not at a point, the Sun I fee not.
  Thus 'tis with fuch, who Grace but now poffeft,
They know not yet, if they are curft or bleft.

V I.

Upon the Flint in the Water.

  This Flint, time out of mind, has there abode,
Where Chryftal Streams make their continual Road ,
Yet it abides a Flint as much as 'twere,
Before it touch'd the Water, or came there.
  Its hard cbduratenefs is not abated,
 'Tis not at all by water penetrated.

Though

Though water hath a foftning vertue in't,
This Stone it can't diffolve, 'caufe 'tis a Flint·
   Yea though it in the water doth remain ;
It doth it's fiery nature ftill retain.
If you oppofe it with it's Oppofit,
At you, yea, in your face it's fire 'twill fpit.

Comparifon.

This Flint an Emblem is of thofe that lye,
   Like ftones, under the Word, until they dye.
It's Chryftal Streams hath not their nature changed
They are not from their Lufts by Grace eftranged.

VII.

Upon the Fish in the Water.

I.

The water is the Fifhes Element :
Take her from thence, none can her death prevent
And fome have faid, who have Tranfgreffors been,
As good not be, as to be kept from fin.

2.

The water is the Fifhes Element :
Leave her but there, and fhe is well content.
So's he who in the path of Life doth plod,
Take all, fays he, let me but have my God.

3.

The water is the Fishes Element:
Her sportings there to her are excellent.
So is God's Service unto Holy men,
They are not in their Element till then.

VIII.

Upon the Swallow.

THis pretty Bird, oh! how she flies and sings!
But could she do so if she had not Wings?
Her Wings, bespeak my Faith, her Songs my Peace,
When I believe and sing, my Doubtings cease.

IX.
Upon the Bee.

THe Bee goes out and Honey home doth bring;
And some who seek that Hony find a sting,
Now wouldst thou have the Hony and be free
From stinging; in the first place kill the Bee.

Comparison.

This Bee an Emblem truly is of sin
Whose Sweet unto a many death hath been.
Now would'st have Sweet from sin, and yet not dye,
Do thou it in the first place mortifie.

X.

X.

Upon the Creed.

I Do believe in God;
And in his only Son;
* as to his Born of a Woman, yet * beget
Godhead. Before the World begun.
I also do believe
That he was crucif'd,
Was dead and buried; and yet
* as to his Believe he * never dy'd.
Godhead. The Third day I believe
He did rise from the dead;
Went up to Heav'n, and is of God
Of all things made the Head.
Also I do believe,
That he from thence shall come,
To judge the quick, the dead, and to
Give unto all just Doom.
Moreover I believe
In God the Holy Ghost;
And that there is an Holy Church,
An universal Host.
Also I do believe,
That sin shall be forgiven;
And that the dead shall rise; and that
The Saints shall dwell in Heaven.

XI.

Upon a low'ring Morning.

WEll, with the day, I fee, the Clouds appear,
 And mix the light with darknefs every where :
This threatning is to Travellers, that go.
Long Journeys, flabby Rain, they'l have or Snow,
 Elfe while I gaze, the Sun doth with his beams
Belace the Clouds, as 'twere with bloody Streams :
This done, they fuddenly do watry grow,
And weep, and pour their tears out where they go.

Comparifon.

Thus 'tis when Gofpel-light doth ufher in
To us, both fenfe of Grace, and fenfe of Sin ;
Yea when it makes fin red with Chrift's blood,
Then we can weep, till weeping does us good.

XII.

Upon over-much Nicenefs.

T'Is much to fee how over-Nice fome are,
 About the Body and Houfhold Affair :
While what's of worth, they flightly pafs it by,
Not doing, or doing it flovenly.

Their

Their houfe muft be well furnifht, be in print ;
Mean while their Soul lies ley, has no good in't.
Its outfide alfo they muft beautifie,
When in it there's fcarce common Honefty.

Their Bodies they muft have trick'd up, and trim
Their infide full of Filth up to the brim.
Upon their cloths there muft not be a fpot,
But is their lives more then one common Blot?

How nice, how coy are fome about their Diet,
That can their crying Souls with Hogs-meat quiet.
All dreft muft to an hair be, elfe 'tis naught,
While of the living bread they have no thought.
Thus for their Outfide they are clean and nice,
While their poor Infide ftinks with fin and vice.

XII.

Meditations upon the Candle.

MAn's like a Candle in a Candleftick,
   Made up of Tallow, and a little Wick ;
And as the Candle is when 'tis not lighted,
So is he who is in his fins benighted.
Nor can a man his Soul with Grace infpire,
More then can Candles fet themfelves on fire.

Candles receive their light from what they are not,
Men Grace from him, for whom at firft they care not,
We manage Candles when they take the fire ;
God men, when he with Grace doth them infpire.
And

And biggeſt Candles give the better light,
As Grace on biggeſt Sinners ſhines moſt, *bright*
The Candle ſhines to make another *ſo*
A Saint unto his Neighbour light ſhould *ſhew*
The blinking Candle we do much deſpiſe,
Saints dim of light are high in no mans eyes.
Again, though it may ſeem to ſome a Riddle,
We uſe to light our Candle at the middle;
True, light doth at the Candles end appear,
And Grace the heart firſt reaches by the Ear.
But 'tis the Wick the fire doth kindle on,
As 'tis the heart that Grace firſt works upon.
Thus both doth faſten upon what's the main,
And ſo their Life and Vigour do maintain.
The Tallow makes the Wick yield to the fire;
And ſinful Fleſh doth make the Soul deſire,
That Grace may kindle on it, in it burn;
So Evil makes the Soul from Evil turn.
But Candles in the wind are apt to flare;
And Chriſt'ans in a Tempeſt to deſpair.
The flame alſo with Smoak attended is;
And in our holy lives there's much amiſs.
Sometimes a Thief will candle-light annoy;
And luſts do ſeek our Graces to deſtroy.
What brackiſh is will make a Candle ſputter;
T'wixt ſin and Grace there's oft a heavy clutter.
Sometimes the light-burns dim, 'cauſe of the ſnuff,
Sometimes it is blown quite out with a puff;
But Watchfulneſs preventeth both theſe evils,
Keeps Candles light and Grace in ſpight of Devils.

Nor

Nor let not ſnuffs nor puffs make us to doubt;
Our Candles may be lighted, though pufft out.
    The Candle in the night doth all excel.
Nor Sun, nor Moon, nor Stars, then ſhine ſo well.
So is the Chriſtian in our Hemiſphere,
Whoſe light ſhews others how their courſe to ſteer.

    When Candles are put out, all's in confuſion;
Where Chriſtians are not, Devils make Intruſion.
Then happy are they who ſuch Candles have,
All others dwell in darkneſs and the Grave.

    But Candles that do blink within the Socket,
And Saints whoſe heads are always in their pocket,
Are much alike; ſuch Candles make us fumble,
And at ſuch Saints, good men and bad do ſtumble.

    Good Candles do'nt offend, except ſore eyes,
Nor hurt unleſs it be the ſilly Flies:
Thus none like burning Candles in the night,
Nor ought to holy living for delight.

    But let us draw towards the Candles end,
The fire, you ſee, doth Wick and Tallow ſpend.
As Grace mans life, until his Glaſs is run,
And ſo the Candle and the Man is done.

    The man now lays him down upon his Bed;
The Wick yields up its fire; and ſo is dead.
The Candle now extinct is, but the man,
By Grace mounts up to Glory, there to ſtand.

XIV

XIV.

Upon the Sacraments.

Two Sacraments I do believe there be,
Baptifm and the Supper of the Lord :
Both Myfteries divine, which do to me,
By Gods appointment, benefit afford :
But fhall they be my God? or fhall I have
Of them fo foul and impious a Thought,
To think that from the Curfe they can me fave?
Bread, Wine, nor Water me no ramfom bought.

XV.

*Upon the Suns RefleƐtion upon the Clouds in a fair Mor-
ning.*

L Ook yonder, ah! Methinks mine eyes do fee,
Clouds edg'd with filver, as fine Garments be !
They look as if they faw that Golden face,
That makes black Clouds moft beautiful with Grace.
Unto the Saints fweet incenfe or their Prayer,
Thefe Smoaky curdled Clouds I do compare.
For as thefe Clouds feem edg'd or lac'd with Gold,
Their Prayers return with Bleffings manifold.

C   XVI.

XVI.

Upon Apparel.

GOd gave us Cloaths to hide our *Nakedness*,
And we by *them*, do it expose to View.
Our Pride, and unclean Minds, *to an excess*,
By our Apparel we to others shew.

XVII.

The Sinner and the Spider.

Sinner.

WHat black? what ugly crawling thing art
Spider. (thou?
I am a Spider ⸺ ⸺

Sinner.
A Spider, Ay, also a filthy Creature.
Spider.
Not filthy as thy self, in Name or Feature :
My Name intailed is to my Creation ;
My Feature's from the God of thy Salvation.
Sinner.
I am a Man, and in God's Image made,
I have a Soul shall neither dye nor fade :
God has possessed me with humane Reason,
Speak not against me, lest thou speakest Treason.

Fo

For if I am the Image of my Maker,
Of Slanders laid on me he is Partaker.

Spider.

I know thou art a Creature far above me,
Therefore I shun, I fear, and also love thee.
But tho thy God hath made thee such a Creature,
Thou haft againſt him often play'd the Traitor.
Thy ſin has fetcht thee down: Leave off to boaſt ;
Nature thou haſt defil'd , God's Image loſt.
Yea thou, thy ſelf a very Beaſt haſt made,
And art become like Graſs, which ſoon doth fade.
Thy Soul, thy Reaſon, yea thy ſpotleſs State.
Sin has ſubjected to th'moſt dreadful fate.
But I retain my primitive condition,
I've all, but what I loſt by thy Ambition.

Sinner.

Thou venom'd thing, I know not what to call thee,
The Dregs of Nature ſurely did befal thee;
Thou waſt made of the Droſs, and Scum of all ;
Man hates thee, doth inſcorn thee Spider call.

Spider.

My Venom s good for ſomething,'cauſe God made it;
Thy Sin has ſpoilt thy Nature, doth degrade it
Of humane Vertues ; therefore tho I fear thee,
I will not, tho I might, deſpiſe and jear thee.
Thou ſayſt I am the very Dregs of Nature,
Thy Sin's the ſpawn of Devils, 'tis no Creature.
Thou ſayſt man hates me, 'cauſe I am a Spider,
Poor man, thou at thy God art a Derider :

My

My venom tendeth to my Preſervation;
Thy pleaſing Follies work out thy Damnation.
Poor man, I keep the rules of my Creation;
Thy ſin has caſt thee headlong from thy Station.
I hurt no body willingly; but thou
Art a ſelf-Murderer: Thou knowſt not how
To do what good is, no thou loveſt evil;
Thou fly'ſt God's Law, adhereſt to the Devil.

Sinner.

Ill-ſhaped Creature there's Antipathy
'Twixt Men and Spiders, 'tis in vain to lie,
I hate thee, ſtand off, if thou doſt come nigh me,
I'll cruſh thee with my foot; I do defie thee.

Spider.

They are ill ſhap't, who warped are by ſin;
Antipathy in thee hath long time bin
To God. No marvel then, if me his Creature
Thou doſt defie, pretending Name and Feature.
But why ſtand off? My Preſence ſhall not throng t
'Tis not my venom, but thy ſin doth wrong the
   Come I will teach thee Wiſdom, do but hear t
I was made for thy profit, do not feer me.
   But if thy God thou wilt not hearken to,
What can the Swallow, Ant, or Spider do?
Yet I will ſpeak, I can but be rejected;
Sometimes great things, by ſmall means are effe
   Hark then; tho man is noble by Creation,
He's lapſed now to ſuch Degeneration;
Is ſo beſotted, and ſo careleſs grown,
As not to grieve, though he has overthrown

Himfelf, and brought to Bondage every thing
Created, from the Spider to the King.
This we poor Senfitives do feel and fee;
For fubject to the Curfe you made us be.
Tread not upon me, neither from me go ;
'Tis man which has brought all the world to Wo.
The Law of my Creation bids me teach thee,
I will not for thy Pride to God impeach thee.
I fpin, I weave, and all to let thee fee,
Thy beft performances but Cob-webs be.
Thy Glory now is brought to fuch an Ebb,
It doth not much excel the Spider's Web.
My Webs becoming fnares aud traps for Flics,
Do fet the wiles of Hell before thine eyes.
Their tangling nature is to let thee fee,
Thy fins (too) of a tangling nature be.
My Den, or Hole, for that 'tis bottomlefs,
Doth of Damnation fhew the Laftingnefs.
My lying quat, until the Fly is catcht,
fhews, fecretly Hell hath thy ruin hatcht.
o that I on her feize, when fhe is taken,
fhew who gathers whom God hath forfaken.
The Fly lies buzzing in my Web to tell
Thee, how the Sinners roar and howl in Hell.
Now fince I fhew thee all thefe Myfteries,
low canft thou hate me; or me Scandalize?

Sinner. :

Well, well, I no more will be a Derider ;
did not look for fuch things from a Spider.

C 3

Spider

Spider.

Come, hold thy peace, what I have yet to say,
If heeded, help thee may another day.
Since I an ugly ven'mous Creature be,
There is some Semblance 'twixt vile Man and Me.
  My wild and heedless Runnings, are like those
Whose ways to ruin do their Souls expose.
Day-light is not my time, I work 'ith' night,
To shew, they are like me who hate the Light.
The slightest Brush will overthrow my house,
To shew false Pleasures are not worse a Louse.
The Maid sweeps one Web down, I make another,
To shew how heedless ones Convictions smother.
My Web is no defence at all to me,
Nor will false Hopes at Judgment be to thee.

Sinner.

O Spider I have heard thee, and do wonder,
A Spider should thus lighten, and thus thunder!

Spider.

  Do but hold still, and I will let thee see,
Yet in my ways more Mysteries there be.
Shall not I do thee good, if I thee tell,
I shew to thee a four-fold way to Hell.
  For since I set my Webs in sundry places,
I shew men go to Hell in divers traces
  One I set in the window, that I might
Shew, some go down to Hell with Gospel-light.
  One I set in a Corner, as you see,
To shew, how some in secret snared be.

Gro

Grofs Webs great ftore I fet in darkfome places,
To fhew, how many fin with brazen faces.

Another Web I fet aloft on high,
To fhew, there's fome profeffing men muft dye.
Thus in my Ways, God Wifdom doth conceal;
And by my ways, that Wifdom doth reveal.

I hide my felf, when I for Flies do wait,
So doth the Devil, when he lays his bait.
If I do fear the lofing of my prey,
I ftir me, and more fnares upon her lay.
This way, and that, her Wings and Legs I tye,
That fure as fhe is catcht, fo fhe muft dye.
But if I fee fhe's like to get away,
Then with my Venom, I her Journey ftay.
All which my ways, the Devil imitates,
To catch men 'caufe he their Salvation hates.

Sinner.

O Spider, thou delight'ft me with thy Skill,
I prethee fpit this Venom at me ftill.

Spider.

I am a Spider, yet I can poffefs
The Palace of a King, where Happinefs
So much abounds. Nor when I do go thither,
Do they ask what, or whence I come, or whether
I make my hafty Travels, no not they ;
They let me pafs, and I go on my way.
I feize the Palace, do with hands take hold
Of Doors, of locks, or bolts ; yea I am bold.

When in, to Clamber up unto the Throne,
And to poffefs it, as if 'twere mine own.

C 4

Nor is there any Law forbidding me
Here to abide, or in this Palace be.
  Yea, If I please I do the highest Stories
Afoond, there fit, and so behold the Glories
My self is compaft with, as if I were
One of the chiefest Courtiers that be there.
  Here Lords and Ladies do come round about me,
With grave Demeanor: Nor do any flout me,
For this my brave Adventure, no not they ;
They come, they go, but leave me there to ftay.
  Now, my Reproacher, I do by all this
Shew how thou may'ft poffefs thy felf of Blifs :
Thou art worfe than a Spider, but take hold
On Chrift the Door, thou fhalt not be controul'd.
By him do thou the Heavenly Palace enter,
None chide thee will for this thy brave Adventure.
  Approach thou then unto the very Throne,
There fpeak thy mind, fear not, the Day's thine own.
Nor Saint nor Angel will thee ftop or ftay ;
But rather tumble blocks out of thy way.
My Venom ftops not me, let not thy Vice
Stop thee ; poffefs thy felf of Paradice.
  Go on, I fay, although thou be a Sinner,
Learn to be bold in Faith of me a Spinner.
This is the way the Glories to poffefs,
And to enjoy what no man can exprefs.
  Sometimes I find the Palace door up lock't ;
And fo my entrance thither as up blockt.
But am I daunted ? No. I here and there
Do feel, and fearch ; fo, if I any where,

At

At any chink or crevife find my way,
I croud,I prefs for paffage, make no ftay ;
And fo, tho difficultly, I attain
The Palace, yea the Throne where Princes reign.
I croud fometimes,as if I'd burft in funder;
And art thou crufh't with ftriving do not wonder.
Some fcarce get in, and yet indeed they enter ;
Knook, for they nothing have that nothing venture.
 Nor will the King himfelf throw dirt on thee,
As thou haft caft Reproaches upon me.
He will not hate thee, O thou foul Backflider!
As thou didft me, becaufe I am a Spider.
 Now, to conclude ; fince I fuch Doctrine bring,
Slight me no more, call me not ugly thing.
God wifdom hath unto the *Pifs-ant* given,
And *Spiders* may teach men the way to Heaven.

Sinner.

Well, my good Spider, I my Errors fee,
I was a fool for railing upon thee.
Thy Nature, Venom, and thy fearful Hue,
Both fhew what Sinners are, and what they do.
 Thy way and works do alfo darkly tell,
How fome men go to Heaven, and fome to Hell.
Thou art my Monitor, I am a Fool ;
They learn may, that to Spiders go to School.

X V I I I.

X V I I I.

Meditatiens upon day before Sun-rifing,

But all this while, where's he whofe Golden rays
Drives night away,and beautifies our days?
Where's he whofe goodly face doth warm and heal,
And fhew us what the darkfome nights conceal?
Where's he that thaws our Ice, drives Cold away?
Let's have him, or we care not for the day.
Thus 'tis with who partakers are of Grace,
There's nought to them like their Redeemers face.

X I X.

Of the Mole in the Ground.

THe Mole's a Creature very fmooth and flick,
She digs i'th'dirt, but 'twill not on her ftick.
So's he who counts this world his greateft gains,
Yet nothing gets but's labour for his pains.
Earth's the Mole's Element, fhe can't abide
To be above ground, dirt heaps are her pride;
And he is like her,who the Wordling plays,
He imitates her in her works, and ways.
Poor filly Mole, that thou fhouldft love to be,
Where thou, nor Sun, nor Moon, nor Stars can fee.
But oh! How filly's he. who doth not care,
So he gets Earth, to have of Heaven a fhare.

X X.

XX,

Of the Cuckow.

Thou Booby, fayſt thou nothing but *Cuckow*?
The *Robin* and the *Wren* can thee out do.
They to us play thorow their little throats,
Not one, but fundry pretty taking Notes.
 But thou haſt Felldws, ſome like thee can do
Little but ſuck our Eggs, and ſing Cuckow.
Thy notes do not *Firſt* welcome in our Spring,
Nor doſt thou it's firſt Tokens to us bring.
Birds leſs then thee by far, like Prophets, do
Tell us 'tis coming, tho not by Cuckow.
Nor doſt thou Summer have away with thee,
Though thou a yauling, bauling Cuckow be.
When thou doſt ceaſe among us to appear,
Then doth our Harveſt bravely crown our year.
 But thou haſt fellows, ſome like thee can do
Little but ſuck our Eggs, and ſing Cuckow.
Since Cuckows forward not our early Spring,
Nor help with notes to bring our Harveſt in :
And ſince while here , ſhe only makes a noiſe,
..So pleaſing unto none as Girls and Boys ;
The Formaliſt we may compare her to,
For he doth ſuck our Eggs and ſing Cuckow,

XXI.

Of the Boy and Butter-Fly.

Behold how eager this our little Boy,
L of this Butter Fly, as if all Joy,
All Profits, Honours, yea and lasting Pleasures,
Were wrapt up in her, or the richest Treasures,
Found in her would be bundled up together,
When all her all is lighter than a feather.
   He hollo's, runs, and cries out here Boys, here,
Nor doth he Brambles or the Nettles fear:
He tumbles at the Mole-Hills, up he gets,
And runs again, as one bereft of wits;
And all this labour and this large Out-cry,
Is only for a silly Butter fly.

Comparison.

This little Boy an Emblem is of those,
Whose hearts are wholly at the World's dispose.
The Butter-fly doth represent to me,
The Worlds best things at best but fading be.
All are but painted Nothings and false Joys,
Like this poor Butter-fly to these our Boys.
   His running thorough Nettles, Thorns and Bryers,
To gratifie his boyish fond desires,
His tumbling over Mole-hills to attain
His end, namely, his Butter-fly to gain;

Doth

Doth plainly shew, what hazards some men run,
To get what will be lost as soon as won.
Men seem in Choice, then children far more wise,
Because they run not after Butter. flies :
When yet alas! for what are empty Toys
They follow Children, like to beardless Boys.

XXII.

Of the Fly at the Candle.

What ails this Fly thus desperately to enter
A Combat with the Candle? will she venture
To claw at light? Away thou silly fly;
Thus doing, thou wilt burn thy wings and dye.
   But 'tis a folly her advice to give,
She'l kill the Candle, or she will not live.
   Slap, says she, at it ; then she makes retreat,
So wheels about and doth her blows repeat.
   Nor doth the Candle let her quite escape,
But gives some little check unto the Ape :
Throws up her heels it doth, so down she falls,
Where she lies sprawling, and for succor calls.
   When she recovers, up she gets again,
And at the Candle comes with might and main
But now behold, the Candle takes the Fly,
And holds her till she doth by burning dye.

Comparison.

Comparison.

This Candle is an Emblem of that Light,
Our Gospel gives in this our darksome night.
The Fly a lively Picture is of those
That hate, and do this Gospel light oppose.
At last the Gospel doth become their snare,
Doth them with burning hands in peices tear.

XXIII.

Upon the Lark and the Fowler

Thou simple Bird what mak'st thou here to play!
Look, there's the Fowler, prethee come away.
Dost not behold the Net? Look there 'tis spread,
Venture a little further thou art dead.
  Is there not room enough in all the Field
For thee to play in, but thou needs must yield
To the deceitful glitt'ring of a Glass,
Plac'd betwixt Nets to bring thy death to pass?
  Bird, if thou art so much for dazling light,
Look, there's the Sun above thee, dart upright?
Thy nature is to soar up to the Sky,
Why wilt thou come down to the nets, and dye?
  Take no heed to the Fowler's tempting Call;
This whistle he enchanteth Birds withal.
Or if thou seest a live Bird in his net,
Believe she's there 'cause thence she cannot get.

Look

Look how he tempteth thee with his Decoy,
That he may rob thee of thy Life, thy Joy:
Come, prethee Bird, I prethee come away,
Why should this net thee take, when 'scape thou may?
    Hadst thou not Wings, or were thy feathers pull'd,
Or wast thou blind or fast asleep wer't lull'd:
The case would somewhat alter, but for thee,
Thy eyes are ope, and thou hast Wings to fee.
    Remember that thy Song is in thy Rise,
Not in thy Fall, Earth's not thy Paradise.
Keep up aloft then, -let thy circuits be
Above, where Birds from Fowlers nets are free.

Comparison

    This Fowler is an Emblem of the Devil,
His Nets and Whistle, Figures of all evil.
His Glass an Emblem is of sinful Pleasure,
And his Decoy, of who counts sin a Treasure.
    This simple Lark's a shadow of a Saint,
Under allurings, ready now to faint.
    This admonisher a true Teacher is,
Whose work's to shew the Soul the snare and bliss.
And how it may this Fowler's net escape,
And not commit upon it self this Rape.

XXIV.

XXIV.

Of the fatted Swine.

Ah, Sirrah! I perceive thou art Corn-fed,
With beft of Hoggs-meat thou art pampered.
Thou wallow'ft in thy fat, up thou art ftal'd,
Art not as heretofore to Hogs-wafh call'd.   (it.
Thine Orts lean Pigs would leap at, might they have
One may fee by their whining how they crave it.
But Hogg, why look'ft fo big? Why doft fo flounce,
So fnort, and fling away, doft now renounce
Subjection to thy Lord, 'caufe he has fed thee?
Thou art yet but a Hogg, of fuch he bred thee.
Lay by thy fnorting, do not look fo big,
What was thy Predeceffor but a Pig.
But come my gruntling, when thou art full fed,
Forth to the Butchers Stall thou muft be led.
Then will an end be put unto thy fnortings,
Unto thy boarifh Looks and hoggifh Sportings;
Then thy fhrill crys will eccho in the air;
Thus will my Pig for all his Greatnefs fare.

Comparifon.

This Emblem fhews, fome men are in this life,
Like full-fed Hoggs prepared for the Knife.
It likewife fhews fome can take no Reproof,
More than the fatted Hogg, who ftands aloof.

Yea

Yea; that they never will for mercy cry,
Till time is paſt, and they for ſin muſt dye.

XXV.

On the riſing of the Sun.

LOok, look, brave *Sol* doth peep up from beneath,
Shews us his golden face, doth on us breath.
He alſo doth compaſs us round with Glories,
Whilſt he aſcends up to his higher Stories.
Where he his Banner over us diſplays,
And gives us light to ſee our Works and Ways.
   Nor are we now, as at the peep of light,
To queſtion, Is it day, or is it night?
The night is gone, the ſhadow's fled away ;
And we now moſt ſure are that it is day.
Our Eyes behold it, and our Hearts believe it,
Nor can the wit of man in this deceive it.
   And thus it is when Jeſus ſhews his face,
And doth aſſure us of his Love and Grace.

XXVL

Upon the promiſing Fruitfulneſs of a Tree.

A Comely ſight indeed it is to ſee,
   A World of Bloſſoms on an Apple-tree.
Yet far more comely would this Tree appear,
If all its dainty blooms young Apples were.

But

But how much more might one upon it fee,
If all would hang there till they ripe fhould be.
But moft of all in Beauty 'twould abound,
If then none worm-eaten could there be found.
　　But we, alas! Do commonly behold
Blooms fall apace, if mornings be but cold.
They (too) which hang till they young Apples are,
By blalting Winds and Vermine take defpair.
Store that do hang, while almoft ripe, we fee
By bluftring Winds are fhaken from the Tree.
So that of many only fome there be,
That grow till they come to Maturity.

Comparifon.

　　This Tree a perfect Emblem is of thofe,
Which God doth plant, which in his Garden grows.
　　It's blafted Blooms are *Motions* unto Good,
Which chill Affections do nip in the bud.
　　Thofe little Apples which yet blafted are,
Shew, fome good *Purpofes*, no good Fruits bare.
　　Thofe fpoilt by Vermin are to let us fee,
How good *Attempts* by bad Thoughts ruin'd be.
　　Thofe which the Wind blows down, while they are
Shew, good *Works* have by Tryal fpoyled been: (green,
　　Thofe that abide, while ripe, upon the Tree,
Shew, in a good man *fome* ripe Fruit *will* be.
　　Behold then how abortive fome Fruits are,
Which at the firft moft promifing appear.

　　　　　　　　　　　　　　The

The Froft,the Wind,the Worm with time doth fhew,
There flows from much Appearance, works but few

XXVII.

On the Poft-boy.

BEhold this Poft-boy, with what hafte and fpeed
He travels on the Road ; and there is need
That he fo does, his Bufinefs call for hafte.
For fhould he in his Journey now be caft,
His Life for that default might hap to go ;
Yea, and the Kingdom come to ruin too.
   Stages are for him fixt, his hour is fet,
He has a Horn to found, that none may let
Him in his hafte, or give him ftop or ftay .
Then Poft-boy blow thy horn, and go thy way.

Comparifon.

This Poft-boy in this hafte an Emblem Is,
Of thofe that are fet out for lafting Blifs.
Nor Pofts that glide the road from day to day,
Have fo much bufinefs, nor concerns as they.
Make clear the road then, Poft-boy found thy horn,
Mifcarry here, and better n'ere been born.

XXVIII.

XXVIII.

Upon the Horfe in the Mill.

HOrfes that work i'th'Mill muft hood-wink't be;
For they'l befick or giddy, if they fee.
But keep them blind enough, and they will go
That way which would a feeing Horfe undo.

Comparifon.

Thus 'tis with thofe that do go *Satan's* Round,
No feeing man can live upon his ground.
Then let us count thofe unto fin inclin'd,
Either befides their wits, bewitch'd or blind.

XXIX

Upon a Ring of Bells.

(weak,

BElls have wide mouths and tongues, but are too
Have they not help, to fing, or talk, or fpeak
But if you move them they will mak't appear,
By fpeaking they'l make all the Town to hear.
When Ringers handle them with Art and Skill,
They then the ears of their Obfervers fill,
With fuch brave Notes, they ting and tang fo well
As to out ftrip all with their ding, dong, Bell.

Comparifon.

Comparison.

These Bells are like the Powers of my Soul;
Their Clappers to the Passions of my mind·
The Ropes by which my Bells are made to tole,
Are Promises (I by experience find.)
My body is the Steeple, where they hang,
My Graces they which do ring ev'ry Bell:
Nor is there any thing gives such a tang,
When by these Ropes these Ringers ring them well.
Let not my Bells these Ringers want, nor Ropes;
Yea let them have room for to swing and sway:
To toss themselves deny them not their Scopes.
Lord! in my Steeple give them room to play.
If they do tole, ring out, or chime all in,
They drown the tempting tinckling Voice of Vice:
Lord! when my Bells have gone, my Soul has bin
As 'twere a tumbling in this Paradice!
Or if these Ringers do the Changes ring,
Upon my Bells, they do such Musick make,
My Soul then (Lord) cannot but bounce and sing,
So greatly her they with their Musick take.
But Boys (my Lusts) into my Belfry go,
And pull these Ropes, but do no Musick make
They rather turn my Bells by what they do,
Or by disorder make my Steeple shake.
Then, Lord! I pray thee keep my Belfry Key,
Let none but Graces meddle with these Ropes:
And when these naughty Boys come, say them Nay,
From such Ringers of Musick there's no hopes.

O!

O Lord! If thy poor Child might have his will,
And might his meaning freely to thee tell ;
He never of this Mufick has his fill,
There's nothing to him like thy ding, dong, Bell.

X X X.

Upon the Thief.

THe Thief, when he doth fteal, thinks he doth gain;
Yet then the greateft Lofs he doth fuftain.
Come Thief, tell me thy Gains, but do not falter.
When fum'd what comes it to more than the Halter?
Perhaps, thoul't fay, the Halter I defie ;
So thou mayft fay, yet by the Halter dye.
Thoul't fay, then there's an end ; no, preth'ee hold,
He was no Friend of thine that thee fo told.
Hear thou the Word of God, that will thee tell,
Without Repentance Thieves muft go to Hell.
But fhould it be as thy falfe Prophet fays,
Yet nought but Lofs doth come by Thievifh ways.
All honeft men will flee thy Company,
Thou liv'ft a Rogue, and fo a Rogue wilt dye.
Innocent boldnefs thou haft none at all,
Thy inward thoughts do thee a Villain call.
Sometimes when thou ly'ft warmly on thy Bed,
Thou art like one unto the Gallows led.
Fear, as a Conftable, breaks in upon thee ;
Thou art as if the Town was up to ftone thee.

If

If Hogs do grunt, or filly Rats do rufle,
Thou art in cônfternations, think'ft a bufle
By men about the door is made to take thee ·
And all becaufe good Confcience doth forfake thee.

Thy cafe is moft deplorably bad ;
Thou fhun'ft to think on't, left thou fhouldft be mad.
Thou art befet with mifchiefs ev'ry way,
The Gallows groaneth for thee ev'ry day.

Wherefore, I prethee Thief, thy Theft forbear,
Confult thy fafety, prethee have a care.
If once thy Head be got within the Noofe,
'Twill be too late a longer Life to chufe.

As to the Penitent thou readeft of,
What's that to them who at Repentance fcoff.
Nor is that Grace at thy Command or Pow'r,
That thou fhouldft put it off till the laft hour.

I prethee Thief think on't, and turn betime;
Few go to Life who do the Gallows clime.

XXXI.

Of the Child with the Bird at the Bush.

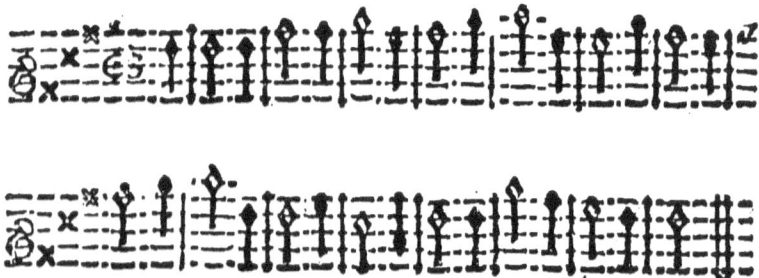

My little Bird, how canſt thou ſit;
  And ſing amidſt ſo many Thorns *!*
Let me but hold upon thee get;
My Love with Honour thee adorns.
  Thou art at preſent little worth;
Five farthings none will give for thee.
But prethee little Bird come forth,
  Thou of more value art to me.
  'Tis true, it is Sun-ſhine to day,
To morrow Birds will have a Storm ;
My pretty one, come thou away,
My Boſom then ſhall keep thee warm.
  Thou ſubject art to cold o'nights,
When darkneſs is thy covering,
At day's thy dangers great by Kites,
How canſt thou then ſit there and ſing ?

Thy

Thy food is fcarce and fcanty too,
Tis Worms and Trafh which thou doft eat;
Thy prefent ftate I pity do,
Come, I'll provide thee better meat.

   I'll feed thee with white Bread and Milk,
And Suger-plumbs, if them thou crave;
I'll cover thee with fineft Silk,
That from the cold I may thee fave.

   My Father's Palace fhall be thine,
Yea in it thou fhalt fit and fing;
My little Bird, if thou'lt be mine,
The whole year round fhall be thy Spring.

   I'll teach thee all the Notes at Court;
Unthought of Mufick thou fhalt play;
And all that thither do refort,
Shall praife thee for it ev'ry day.

   I'll keep thee fafe from Cat and Cur,
No manner o'harm fhall come to thee;
Yea, I will be thy Succourer,
My Bofom fhall thy Cabbin be.
But lo, behold, the Bird is gone;
Thefe Charmings would not make her yield:
The Child's left at the Bufh alone,
The Bird flies yonder o'er the Field.

Comparifon.

   This Child of Chrift an Emblem is;
The Bird to Sinners I compare:
The Thorns are like thofe Sins of his,
Which do furround him ev'ry where.

Her Songs, her Food, and Sun-ſhine day,
An Emblem's of thoſe fooliſh Toys,
Which to Deſtruction lead the way,
The fruit of worldly, empty Joys.

    The Argnments this Child doth chuſe,
To draw to him a Bird thus wild,
Shews Chriſt familiar Speech doth uſe,
To make's to him be reconciled.

    The Bird in that ſhe takes her Wing,
To ſpeed her from him after all:
Shews us, vain Man loves any thing,
Much better than the Heav'nly Call.

XXXII.

Of Moſes and his Wife.

THis *Moſes* was a fair and comely man;
   His wife a ſwarthy Ethiopian :
Nor did his Milk-white Boſom change her Skin;
She came out thence as black as ſhe went in.
Now *Moſes* was a type of *Moſes* Law,
His Wife likewiſe of one that never ſaw
Another way unto eternal Life ;
There's Myſt'ry then in *Moſes* and his Wife.

    The Law is very Holy, Juſt and good,
And to it is eſpouſ'd all Fleſh and Blood :
But this its Goodneſs it cannot beſtow,
On any that are wedded thereunto.

                  Therefore

Therefore as *Moses* Wife came fwarthy in,
And went out from him without change of Skin:
So he that doth the Law for Life adore,
Shall yet by it be left a Black-a-more.

XXXIII.

Upon the barren Fig-tree in God's Vineyard

What barren here! in this, fo good a foyl?
The fight of this doth make God's heart recoyl
From giving thee his Bleffing. Barren Tree,
Bear Fruit, elfe thine end will curfed be!
 Art thou not planted by the water fide?
Know'ft not thy Lord by Fruit is glorifi'd?
The Sentence is, cut down the barren Tree:
Bear Fruit, or elfe thine End will curfed be!
 Haft not been dig'd about, and dunged too,
Will neither Patience, nor yet Dreffing do?
The Executioner is come, O Tree,
Bear Fruit, or elfe thine End will curfed be!
 He that about thy Roots takes pains to dig,
Would if on thee were found but one good Fig,
Preferve thee from the Axe: But barren Tree,.
Bear Fruit, or elfe thy End will curfed be!
 The utmoft end of Patience is at hand,
'Tis much if thou much longer here doth ftand.
O Cumber-ground, thou art a barren Tree,
Bear Fruit, or elfe thine End will curfed be!

Thy ſtanding nor thy name will help at all,
When fruitful Trees are ſpared thou muſt fall.
The Axe is laid unto thy Roots.O Tree !·
Bear fruit, or elſe thine End will curſed be !

XXXIIII.

Of the Roſe-buſh.

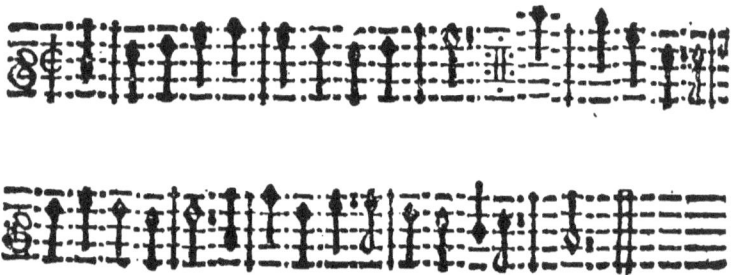

THis homely Buſh doth to mine eyes expoſe,
A very fair, yea comely, ruddy, *Roſe.*
This *Roſe* doth alſo bow its head to me,
Saying,come, pluck me, I thy Roſe will be.
Yet offer I to gather Roſe or Bud,
Ten to one but the Buſh will have my Blood.
This looks like a Trappan,or a Decoy,
To offer, and yet ſnap who would enjoy.
Yea, the more eager on't, the more in danger,
Be he the Maſter of it, or a Stranger.
Buſh, why doſt bear a Roſe? If none muſt have it,
Why doſt expoſe it, yet claw thoſe that crave it?

Ar

Art become freakish ? Doft the Wanton play,
Or doth thy tefty humour tend this way ?

Comparifon.

This Rofe God's Son is, with his ruddy Looks.
But what's the *Bufh* ? Whofe pricks, like Tenter-
Do fcratch and claw the fineft Ladies hands, (hooks.
Or rent her Cloths, if fhe too near it ftands.
  This *Bufh* an Emblem is of *Adam's* race
Of which Chrift came, when he his Father's Grace
Commended to us in his crimfon Blood,
While he in Sinners ftead and Nature ftood.
  Thus *Adam's* Race did bear this dainty Rofe,
And doth the fame to *Adam's* Race expofe :
But thofe of *Adam's* Race which at it catch,
Adam's Race will them prick and claw and fcratch.

XXXV.

Of the going down of the Sun.

  What, haft thou run thy Race ? Art going down ?
Thou feemeft angry, why doft on us frown ?
Yea wrap thy head with Clouds, and hide thy face,
As threatning to withdraw from us thy Grace ?
Oh leave us not ! when once thou hid'ft thy head,
Our Horizon with darknefs will be fpread.
Tell's, who hath thee offended ? Turn again :
Alas ! too late Entreaties are in vain !

                     Comparifon.

Comparison.

Our Gospel has had here a Summers day ;
But in its Sun-shine we, like Fools, did play.
Or else fall out, and with each other wrangle,
And did in stead of work not much but jangle.
   And if our Sun seems angry, hides his face,
Shall it go down, shall Night possess this place?
Let not the voice of night-Birds us afflict,
And of our mis-spent Summer us convict.

XXXVI.

Upon the Frog.

THe Frog by Nature is both damp and cold,
   Her Mouth is large, her Belly much will hold:
She sits somewhat ascending, loves to be
Croaking in Gardens, tho unpleasantly.

Comparison.

   The Hyppocrite is like unto this Frog ;
As like as is the Puppy to the Dog.
He is of nature cold. his Mouth is wide,
To prate, and at true Goodness to deride,
He mounts his Head, as if he was above
   The World, when yet 'tis that which has his Love.

And

And though he seeks in Churches for to croak,
He neither loveth Jesus, nor his Yoak.

XXXVII.

Upon the whipping of a Top.

'Tis with the Whip the Boy sets up the Top,
   The Whip makes it run round upon it's Toe;
TheWhip makes it hither and thither hop:
Tis with the Whip, the Top is made to go.

Comparison.

Our Legalist is like unto this Top,
Without a Whip, he doth not Duty do.
Let *Moses* whip him, he will skip and hop;
Forbear to whip, he'l neither stand nor go.

XXXVIII.

Upon the Pismire.

Must we unto the Pis-mire go to School,
   To learn of her, in Summer to provide
For Winter next ensuing; Man's a Fool,
Or silly Ants would not be made his Guide.
   But Sluggard, is it not a shame for thee,
To be out-done by Pis-mires? Prethee hear:

Their.

Their Works (too) will thy Condemnation be,
When at the Judgment Seat thou shalt appear.
But since thy God doth bid thee to her go,
Obey, her ways consider, and be wise.
The Pifs-ants tell thee will what thou must do,
And set the way to Life before thine eyes. ·

XXXIX.

Upon the Beggar.

HE wants, he asks, he pleads his Poverty,
They within doors do him an Alms deny.
He doth repeat and aggravate his Grief;
But they repulse him, give him no relief.
He begs, they say, be gone; he will not hear,
But coughs, sighs and make signs, he still is there
They disregard him, he repeats his groans;
They still say nay, and he himself bemoans.
The grow more rugged, they call him Vagrant;
He cries the shriller, trumpets out his want.
At last when they perceive he'll take no Nay,
An Alms they give him without more delay.

Comparison.

This Beggar doth resemble them that pray,
To God for Mercy, and will take no Nay.
But wait, and count that all his hard Gain-says,
Are nothing else, but fatherly Delays.

Then.

Then imitate him, praying Souls, and cry :
There's nothing like to Importunity.

X L.

Upon an Instrument of Musick in an unskilful Hand.

SUppose a Viol, Cittern, Lute, or Harp,
  Committed unto him that wanteth Skill ;
Can he by Strokes. suppose them flat or sharp,
The Ear of him that hears with Musick fill ?
  No, no, he can do little else then scrape,
Or put all out of tune, or break a string :
Or make thereon a mutt'ring like an Ape,
Or like one which can neither say nor sing.

Comparison.

The unlearn'd Novices in things Divine,
With this unskill'd Musician I compare.
For such, instead of making Truth to shine,
Abuse the Bible, and unsavoury are.

X L I.

Upon the Horse and his Rider

THere's one rides very sagely on the Road,
  Shewing that he affects the gravest Mode.
Another rides Tantivy, or full Trot,
To shew, much Gravity he matters not.

Lo,

Lo, here comes one amain, he rides full speed,
Hedge, Ditch, nor Myry Bog, he doth not heed.
One claws it up Hill without stop or check,
Another down, as if he'd break his Neck.
Now ev'ry Horse has his especial Guider;
Then by his going you may know the Rider.

Comparison

Now let us turn our Horse into a Man,
His Rider to a Spirit, if we can :
Then let us by the Methods of the Guider,
Tell ev'ry Horse how he should know his Rider.

Some go as Men direct in a right way,
Nor are they suffered to go astray :
As with a Bridle they are governed,
And kept from Paths, which lead unto the dead.
Now this good man has his especial Guider;
Then by his going let him know his Rider.

Some go as if they did not greatly care,
Whether of Heaven or Hell they should be Heir.
The Rein it seems as laid upon their Neck,
They seem to go their way without a check.
Now this man too has his especial Guider;
And by his going he may know his Rider.

Some again run, as if resolv'd to dye,
Body and Soul to all Eternity:

Good

ood Counſel they by no means can abide;
hey'l have their courſe, whatever them betide.
Now theſe poor Men have their eſpecial Guider;
'ere they not Fools they ſoon might know their Rider.

There's one makes head againſt all Godlineſs,
hoſe (too) that do profeſs it he'l diſtreſs :
;'l taunt and ſtout, if Goodneſs doth appear,
ıd at its Countenancers mock and jear.
Now this man (too) has his eſpecial Guider;
And by his going he might know his Rider.

XLII.

Upon the Sight of a Pound of Candles falling to the
Ground.

ıUt be the Candles down, and ſcatt'red too,
ı Some lying here, ſome there? What ſhall we do?
ıld, light the Candle there that ſtands on high,
you may find the other Candles by.
ght that, I ſay, and ſo take up the Pound,
ıu did let fall, and ſcatter on the Ground.

Compariſon.

The fallen Candles to us intimate,
ıe bulk of God's Elect in their lapſt State.
heir lying ſcatt'red in the dark may be,
ı ſhew by Man's lapſt State his Miſery,

The

The Candle that was taken down, and lighted,
Thereby to find them fallen, and benighted,
Is Jefus Chrift: God by his Light doth gather
Who he will fave, and be unto a Father.

X L.I I I.

Of Fowls flying in the Air.

MEthinks I fee a Sight moft excellent,
  All Sorts of Birds fly in the Firmament:
Some great, fome fmall, all of a divers kind,
Mine Eye affecting, pleafant to my Mind.
Look how they tumble in the wholefom Air,
Above the World of Wordlings, and their care.
  And as they divers are in Bulk and Hue,
So are they in their way of flying too.
  So many Birds, fo many various things,
Tumbling i'th'Element upon their Wings.

Comparifon.

  Thefe Birds are Emblems of thofe men, that fhall
Ere long poffefs the Heavens, their All in All.
  They are each of a divers fhape, and kind;
To teach, we of all Nations there fhall find,
  They are fome great, fome little, as we fee;
To fhew, fome great, fome fmall, in Glory be.
  Their flying diverfly, as we behold;
Do fhew Saints Joys will there be manifold.

Some

Some glide, some mount, some flutter, and some do,
In a mixt way of flying, glory too.
And all to shew each Saint, to his content,
Shall roul and tumble in that Firmament.

XLIV.

Upon a Penny Loaf.

THy Price one Penny is, in time of Plenty;
  In Famine doubled 'tis, from one to twenty:
Yea, no man knows what Price on thee to set,
When there is but one Penny Loaf to get.

Comparison.

THis Loaf's an Emblem of the Word of God,
  A thing of low Esteem, before the Rod
Of Famine smites the Soul with Fear of Death:
But then it is our All, our Life, our Breath.

XLV.

Upon the Vine-tree.

WHat is the Vine, more than another Tree,
  Nay most, than it, more tall, more comly be?
What Work-man thence will take a Beam or Pin,
To make ought which may be delighted in?

It's

It's Excellency in it's Fruit doth lie.
A fruitless Vine! It is not worth a Fly.

Comparison.

What are Professors more than other men?
Nothing at all.   Nay, there's not one in ten,
Either for Wealth, or Wit, that may compare,
In many things, with some that Carnal are.
Good are they, if they mortifie their Sin;
But without that they are not worth a Pin.

XLVI

The Boy and Watch-maker.

THis Watch my Father did on me bestow,
A Golden one it is, but 'twill not go,
Unless it be at an Uncertainty;
But as good none, as one to tell a Lye.
When 'tis high Day, my Hand will stand at nin
I think there's no man's Watch so bad as mine.
Sometimes 'tis sullen, 'twill not go at all,
And yet 'twas never broke, nor had a Fall.

Watch-maker.

Your Watch, tho it be good, through want of sk
May fail to do according to your will.

Suppofe the Ballance, Wheels, and Spring be good,
And all things elfe, unlefs you underftood
To manage it, as Watches ought to be,
Your Watch will ftill be at Uncertainty.
Come, tell me, do you keep it from the Duft?
Yea wind it alfo duly up you muft.
Take heed (too) that you do not ftrain the String;
You muft be circumfpect in ev'ry thing.
Or elfe your Watch, were it as good again,
Would not with Time, and Tide you entertain.

Comparifon.

This Boy an Emblem is of a Convert;
His Watch of th'work of Grace within his heart.
The Watch-maker is Jefus Chrift our Lord,
His Counfel, the Directions of his Word.
Then Convert, if thy heart be out of frame,
Of this Watch-maker learn to mend the fame.
Do not lay ope'thy heart to Worldly Duft,
Nor let thy Graces over-grow with Ruft.
Be oft renew'd in th' Spirit of thy mind,
Or elfe uncertain thou thy Watch wilt find.

XLVII.

Upon the Boy and his Paper of Plumbs.

WHat haft thou there, my pretty Boy?
Plumbs? How? Yes, Sir, a Paper full.
I thought 'twas fo, becaufe with Joy
Thou didft them out thy Paper pull.

E 4

The

The Boy goes from me, eats his Plumbs,
Which he counts better of than Bread :
But by and by he to me comes,
With nought but Paper and the Thread.

Comparison.

This Boy an Emblem is of such,
Whose Lot in worldly things doth lie:
Glory they in them ne'er so much,
Their pleasant Springs will soon be dry.
 Their Wealth, their Health, Honours and Life,
Will quickly to a period come ;
If for these, is their only Strife,
They soon will not be worth a Plumb.

XLVIII.

Upon a Looking-glass.

IN this, see thou thy Beauty, hast thou any :
 Or thy defects, should they be few or many.
Thou mayst (too) here thy Spots and Freckles see,
Hast thou but Eyes, and what their Numbers be.
But art thou blind, there is no Looking Glass,
Can shew thee thy defects, thy Spots, or Face.

Comparison.

Comparison.

Unto this Glaſs we may compare the Word,
For that to man advantage doth afford,
(Has he a Mind to know himſelf and State;)
To ſee what will be his Eternal Fate.
  But without Eyes, alas ! How can he ſee ?
Many that ſeem to look here, blind Men be.
This is the Reaſon, they ſo often read,
Their Judgment there, and do it nothing dread.

XLIX.

Upon a Lanthorn.

THe Lanthorn is to keep the Candle Light,
   When it is windy, and a darkſome Night.
O.dain'd it alſo was, that men might ſee
By Night their Day, and ſo in ſafety be.

Comparison.

Compare we now our Lanthorn to the man,
That has within his heart a Work of Grace.
As for another let him, if he can,
Do as this Lanthorn, in its time and place:
  Profeſs the Faith, and thou a Lanthorn art:
But yet if Grace has not poſſeſſed thee:

Thou.

Thou want'ſt this Candle Light within thy heart,
And art none other, than dark Lanthorns be.

L.

Of the Love of Chriſt.

THe love of Chriſt, poor I! may touch upon
But 'tis unſearchable. Oh! There is none
It's large Dimenſions can comprehend,
Should they dilate thereon, World without end.
When we had ſinned, in his Zeal he ſware,
That he upon his back our Sins would bear.
And ſince unto Sin is entailed Death,
He vowed, for our Sins he'd loſe his Breath.
He did not only ſay, vow, or reſolve,
But to Aſtoniſhment did ſo involve
Himſelf, in man's diſtreſs and miſery,
As for, and with him, both to live and dye.
To his eternal Fame, in Sacred Story,
We find that he did lay aſide his Glory.
Step'd from the Throne of higheſt Dignity;
Become poor Man, did in a Manger lie;
Yea was beholding unto his for Bread;
Had, of his own, not where to lay his Head.
Tho rich, he did, for us, become thus poor,
That he might make us rich for evermore.
Nor was this but the leaſt of what he did;
But the outſide of what he ſuffered
God made his Bleſſed Son under the Law;
Under the Curſe, which, like the Lyon's Paw,

Did rent and tear his Soul, for mankinds Sin,
More than if we for it in Hell had bin.
His Crys, his Tears, and Bloody Agony,
The nature of his Death, doth testify.

Nor did he of Constraint himself thus give,
For Sin, to death, that man might with him live.
He did do what he did most willingly,
He sung, and gave God Thanks, that he must dye.

But do Kings use to dye for Captive Slaves?
Yet we were such, when Jesus dy'd to save's.

Yea, when he made himself a Sacrifice,
It was that he might save his Enemies.

And, tho he was provoked to retract
His blest Resolves, for such, so good an Act,
By the abusive Carriages of those
That did both him, his Love, and Grace oppose:
Yet he, as unconcerned with such things,
Goes on, determines to make Captives Kings.
Yea, many of his Murderers he takes
Into his Favour, and them Princes makes.

LI.

Of the Horse and Drum.

SOme Horses will, some can't endure the Drum,
But snort and flounce, if it doth near them come.
They will, nor Bridle nor Rider obey,
But head strong be, and fly out of the way.

These

These skittish Jades, that can't this noise abide,
Nor will be rul'd by him that doth them ride;
I do compare those our Professors to,
Which start from Godliness in Tryals do.
To these, the threats that are against them made,
Are like this Drum to this our starting Jade.
They are offended at them and forsake
Christ, of whose ways they did Profession make.
But, as I said, there other Horses be,
That from a Drum will neither start, nor flee.
Let Drummers beat a Charge, or what they will,
They'l nose them, face them, keep their places still.
They fly not when they to those rattlings come,
But like War-Horses do endure the Drum.

LII.

On the Kackling of a Hen.

THe Hen so soon as she an Egg doth lay,
(Spreads the Fame of her doing, what she may.)
About the Yard she kackling now doth go,
To tell what 'twas she at her Nest did do.

Just thus it is with some Professing men,
If they do ought that good is, like our Hen,
They can't but kackle on't, where 'ere they go,
What their right hand doth, their left hand must
(know.

LIII.

LIII.

Upon an Hour-Glass.

THis Glafs when made, was by the Work mans
   The Sum of fixty minutes to fulfill.   (Skill,
Time more, nor lefs, by it will out be fpun,
But juft an Hour, and then the Glafs is run.

Man's Life, we will compare unto this Glafs,
The Number of his Months he cannot pafs ;
But when he has accomplifhed his day,
He, like a Vapour, vanifheth away.

LIV.

Upon the Chalk-ftone.

'THis Stone is white, yea, warm, and alfo foft,
   Eafie to work upon, unlefs 'tis naught.
It leaves a white Impreffion upon thofe ,
Whom it doth touch, be they it's Friends or Foes.

The Child of God, is like to this Chalk-ftone,
White in his Life, eafily wrought upon :
Warm in Affections, apt to leave imprefs,
On whom he deals with, of true Godlinefs.
   He is no fulling Coal, nor daubing Pitch,
Nor one of whom men catch the Scab, or Itch ;
                               But

But such who in the Law of God doth walk,
Tender of heart, in Life whiter than Chalk.

LV.

Upon a Stinking Breath.

DOth this proceed from an infected Air? (Fare?
Or from man's common, sweet and wholesome
It comes from a foul Stomack, or what's worse,
Ulcerous Lungs, Teeth, or a private Curse.

To this, I some mens Notions do compare,
Who seem to breathe in none but Scripture Air.
They suck it in, but breathe it out again,
So putrified, that it doth scarce retain
Any thing of its native Excellence.
It only serves to fix the Pestilence
Of their delusive Notions, in the mind
Of the next foolish Proselyte they find.

LVI.

Upon Death.

DEath's a cold Comforter to Girls and Boys,
Who wedded are unto their Childish Toys:
More Grim he looks upon our lustful Youth, (Truth
Who, against Knowledge, slight God's saving

But moſt of all, he diſmal is to thoſe,
Who once profeſs'd the Truth, they now oppoſe.
  Death has a Dart, a Sting, which Poyſon is,
As all will find, who do of Glory miſs.
This Sting is Sin, the Laws it's Strength, and he,
Or they, will find it ſo, who damned be.
  True, Jeſus Chriſt, indeed, did Death deſtroy,
For thoſe who worthy are, him to enjoy.
He waſhes them in's Blood from ev'ry Sin
They'r guilty of, or ſubject to hath bin.
So here's, nor Sting, nor Law, nor Death to kill,
And yet Death always, ſome men torment will.
  But this ſeems Het'rodox or Myſtery,
For Death to live to ſome, to ſome to dye;
Yet 'tis ſo, when God doth man's Sin forgive,
Death dies, but where 'tis charged, Death doth live.

LVIL

Upon the Snail.

SHe goes but ſoftly, but ſhe goeth ſure,
  She ſtumbles not, as ſtronger Creatures do :
Her Journeys ſhorter, ſo ſhe may endure,
Better than they which do much further go.
  She makes no noiſe, but ſtilly ſeizeth on
The Flow'r or Herb, appointed for her food:
The which ſhe quietly doth feed upon,
While others range, and gare, but find no good.

And

And tho fhe doth but very foftly go,
How ever 'tis not faft, nor flow but fure;
And certainly they that do travel fo,
The prize they do aim at, they do procure.

Comparifon.

Although they feem not much to ftir, lefs go,
For Chrift that hunger, or from Wrath, that flee;
Yet what they feek for, quickly thy come to,
Tho it doth feem the fartheft off to be.
One Act of Faith doth bring them to that Flow'r,
They fo long for, that they may eat and live;
Which to attain is not in others Pow'r,
Tho for it a King's Ranfom they would give.
Then let none faint, nor be at all difmaid,
That Life by Chrift do feek, they fhall not fail
To have it, let them nothing be afraid;
The Herb, and Flow'r is eaten by the Snail.

LVIII.

Of the Spoufe of Chrift.

(nefs,
VVHo's this that cometh from the Wildor-
Like Smoaky Pillars, thus perfumed with
Leaning upon her deareft in Diftrefs, (Myrrhe
Led into's Bofom, by the Comforter?

She's

She's clothed with the Sun, crown'd with twelve
The spotted Moon her Footstool he hath made.(Stars,
The Dragon her assaults, fills her with Jarrs,
Yet rests she under her Beloved's Shade.

But whence was she? What is her Pedigree ?
Was not her Father, a poor *Amorite* ?
What was her Mother, but as others be,
A poor, a wretched and sinful *Hittite* !

Yea, as for her, the day that she was born,
As loathsome, out of doors, they did her cast ;
Naked, and Filthy, Stinking, and forlorn:
This was her Pedigree from first to last.

Nor was she pittied in this Estate ;
All let her lie polluted in her Blood:
None her Condition did commiserate,
Their was no Heart that sought to do her good.

Yet she unto these Ornaments is come,
Her Breasts are fashioned, her Hair is grown ;
She is made Heiress of the best Kingdom ;
All her Indignities away are blown.

Cast out she was, but now she home is taken,
Naked (sometimes) but now you see she's clo'd;
Now made the Darling, though before forsaken.,
Bare-foot, but now, as Princes Daughters, shod.

Instead of Filth. she now has her Perfumes,
Instead of Ignominy. her Chains of Gold:
Instead of what the Beauty most consumes,
Her Beauty's perfect, lovely to behold.

Those that attend, and wait upon her, be
Princes of Honour, cloth'd in white Aray ,

F

Upon

Upon her Head's a Crown of Gold, and she
Eats Wheat, Honey, and Oil, from day to day.
    For her Beloved, he's the High'st of all,
The only Potentate , the King of Kings :
Angels, and Men, do him *Jehovah* call,
And from him, Life, and Glory, always springs.
    He's white, and ruddy, and of all the Chief ;
His Head, his Locks, his Eyes, his Hands, and Feet,
Do for Compleatness out-go all Belief ;
His cheeks like Flowers are, his Mouth's most sweet.
    As for his Wealth he is made Heir of all,
What is in Heav'n, what is on Earth, is his :
And he this Lady, his Joynt-Heir, doth call,
Of all that shall be, or at present is.
    Well Lady, well, God has been good to thee,
Thou, of an Out-cast, now art made a Queen.
Few or none may with thee compared be ;
A Beggar made thus high is seldome seen.
Take heed of Pride, remember what thou art,
By Nature, tho thou hast in Grace a share :
Thou in thy self doth yet retain a part
Of thine own Filthiness, wherefore beware.

LIX.

Upon a Skilful Player on an Instrument.

HE that can play well on an Instrument,
    Will take the Ear, and captivate the Mind,
With Mirth, or Sadness : For that *it* is bent
Thereto as Musick, in it, place doth find.

But

But if one hears that hath therein no skill,
(As often Mufick lights of fuch a chance)
Of its brave Notes, they foon be weary will ;.
And there are fome can neither fing nor dance.

Comparifon.

Unto him that thus skilfully doth play,
God doth compare a Gofpel-Minifter,
That rightly preacheth (and doth Godly pray)
Applying truly what doth thence infer.
   This man, whether of Wrath or Grace he preach,.
So skilfully doth handle ev'ry Word ;
And by his Saying, doth the heart fo reach,
That it doth joy or figh before the Lord. '
   But fome there be. which, as the Bruit, doth lie
Under the Word, without the leaft advance
God-ward : Such do defpife the Miniftry,
They weep not at it, neither to it dance.

L X.

Upon Fly-blows.

THere is good Meat provided for man's Health.
   To this the Flefh fly comes, as twere by Stealth.
Bloweth thereon, and fo *Be-maggots* it,
As that it is, tho' wholfome, quite unfit
For queazy Stomachs, they muft pafs it by :
Now is not this a prejudicial Fly?

Comparifon.

Comparison.

Let this good Meat, good Doctrine fignify,
And call him which reproaches it, this Fly.
For as this Flesh-fly blows this wholfome meat,
That it the queazy Stomach cannot eat:
So they which do good Doctrine fcandalize,
Prefent it unto fome in fuch Difguize;
That they cannot accept, nor with it clofe,
But flight it, and themfelves to Death expofe.
Reproach it then, thou art a mauling Club,
This Fly, yea, and the Son of *Belzebub*.

L X I.

Of Man by Nature

FRom God he's a Back flider,
  Of Ways, he loves the wider;
With Wickednefs a Sider,
More Venom than a Spider.
   In Sin he's a Confider,
A Make-bate, and Divider;
Blind Reafon is his Guider,
The Devil is his Rider.

LXII.

Of Phyfick:

PUrging Phyfick,taken to heat or cool,
Worketh by Vomit, Urine, Sweat or Stool ;
But if it worketh not, then we do fear
The danger's great, the Perfon's Death is near.
If more be added , and it worketh not ;
And more, and yet the fame's the Patients Lot.
All hope of Life from Standers-by is fled,
The Party fick is counted now as dead.

Comparifon.

Count ye the Sick, one that's not yet converted,
Impenitent, Incredulous, Hard-hearted :
In whom vile Sin is fo predominant,
And the Soul in it's Acts fo converfant ;
That like one with Difeafes over-run,
This man with it at prefent is undone.
Now let the Phyfick be the Holy Word,
(The Bleffed Doctrine of our Deareft Lord.)
And let the Dofes to the Patient given
Be, by Directions of the God of Heaven.
Convincing Sermons, fharp and found Rebukes,
Let them be Beggars,Knights,Lords,Earls or Dukes:
You muft not fpare them, Life doth lie at Stake,
And dye they will, if Phyfick they don't take.

If thefe do finely work, then let them have
Directions unto him that can them fave.
Lay open then the Riches of his Grace,
And Merits of his Blood before their Face.
Shew them likewife, how free he is to give
His Juftice unto them, that they may live.
If they will doubt, and not your Word believe,
Shew them, at prefent they have a Reprieve;
On purpofe they might out their Pardon fue,
And have the Glory of it in their view.
   Inftances of this Goodnefs fet before,
Their Eyes, that they this Mercy may adore.
And if this Phyfick taken worketh well,
Fear not a Cure, you fave a Soul from Hell.
   But if thefe Dofes do not kindly work,
If the Difeafe ftill in their Mind doth lurk :
If they inftead of throwing up their Vice,
Do vomit up the Word, loath Paradice :
Repeat the Potion, them new Dofes give,
Which are much ftronger, perhaps they may live :
But if they ferve thefe as they ferv'd the reft,
And thou perceiv'ft it is not to them Bleft :
If they remain incorrigible ftill,
And will the Number of their Sins fulfill ;
The Holy Text doth fay that they muft dye ;
Yea, and be damned without Remedy.

LXIII.

LXIII.

Upon a Pair of Spectacles.

SPectacles are for Sight, and not for Shew,
  Necessity doth Spectacles commend ;
Was't not for need, there is but very few,
That would for wearing Spectacles contend.
  We use to count them very dark indeed,
Whose Eyes so dim are, that they cannot be
Helped by Spectacles ; such men have need
A Miracle be wrought to make them see.

Comparison.

Compare Spectacles to God's Ordinances,
For they present us with his Heav'nly Things ;
Which else we could not see for hinderances,
That from our dark and foolish Nature springs.
  If this be so, what shall we say of them,
Who at God's Ordinances scoff and jear ?
They do those Blessed Spectacles condemn,
By which Divine Things are made to appear.

LXIV.

Upon our being so afraid of small Creatures.

MAn by Creation was made Lord of all,
  But now he is become an Underling ;
He thought he should a gained by his Fall,
But lost his Head-ship over ev'ry thing.

                          What !

What ! What ! A humane Creature and afraid
Of Frogs, Dogs, Cats, Rats, Mice, or such like Crea-
This fear of thine has fully thee betraid,   ture?
Thou art Back-slid from God, to him a Traytor.
How by his Fall is stately Man decay'd ?
Nor is it in his hand now to renew him,
Of things dismaid, at him, he is afraid ;
Worms, Lice, Flies, Mice ; Yea Vanities subdue him.

L X V.

Upon our being afraid of the Apparition of Evil Spirits.

Some fear more the Appearance of the Devil,
Than the Commission of the greatest Evil.
They start, they tremble, if they think he's near,
But can't be pleased unless Sin appear.
These Birds, the Fowler's Presence doth afright,
To be among his Lime-twigs, they delight.
But, just men who have with the Devil bin,
Have been more safe, than some in Heav'n with Sin,

L X V I.

Upon the Disobedient Child.

CHildren become, while little, our delights,
When they grow bigger, they begin to fright's
Their sinful Nature prompts them to rebel,
And to delight in Paths that lead to Hell.

Their

Their Parents Love, and Care, they overlook,
As if Relation had them quite forfook.
They take the Counfels of the Wanton's rather,
Then the moft grave Inftructions of a Father.
They reckon Parents ought to do for them,
Tho they the Fifth Commandement contemn.
They fnap, and fnarl, if Parents them controul,
Tho but in things, moft hurtful to the Soul.
They reckon they are Mafters, and that we,
Who Parents are, fhould to them Subject be !
If Parents fain would have a hand in chufing,
The Children have a heart will in refufing.
They'l by wrong doings, under Parents, gather
And fay, it is no Sin to rob a Father,
They'l joftle Parents out of place and Pow'r,
They'l make themfelves the Head, and them devour,
How many Children, by becoming Head,
Have brought their Parents to a peice of Bread:
Thus they who at the firft were Parents Joy,
Turn that to Bitternefs, themfelves deftroy.

But Wretched Child, how canft thou thus requite
Thy Aged Parents, for that great delight
They took in thee, when thou, as helplefs lay
In their Indulgent Bofoms day by day ?
Thy Mother, long before fhe brought thee forth,
Took care thou fhould'ft want, neither Food, nor
Thy Father glad was at his very heart,   (Cloth.
Had he, to thee, a Portion to impart.
Comfort they promifed themfelves in thee,
But thou, it feems, to them a Grief wil't be,

How

How oft ! How willingly brake they their Sleep,
If thou , their Bantling, didſt but whinch or weep.
Their Love to thee was ſuch, they could have giv'n,
That thou might'ſt live, almoſt, their part of Heav'n.
   But now, behold, how they rewarded are !
For their Indulgent Love, and tender Care,
All is forgot, this Love he doth deſpiſe,
They brought this Bird up to pick out their Eyes.

LXVII.

Upon the Boy on his Hobby-horſe.

L Ook how he ſwaggers, cocks his Hat, and rides,
   How on his Hobby-horſe, himſelf he prides :
He looketh grim, and up his Head doth toſs,
Says he'l ride over's with his Hobby-horſe.

Compariſon.

   Some we ſee mounted upon the Conceit
That their Wit, Wealth, or Beauty is ſo great :
But few their Equals may with them compare,
Who yet more Godly, Wiſe, and Honeſt are.
Behold how huff, how big they look ; how high
They lift their heads, as if they'd touch the Skie :
Nor will they count theſe things, for Chriſt, a loſs
So long as they do ride this Hobby-horſe.

.How

LXVIII.

LXVIII

Upon the Image in the Eye.

VVHo looks upon another ftedfaftly,
  Shall forthwith have his Image in his eye,
Doft thou believe in Jefus? (Haft that Art ?)
Thy Faith will place his Image in thy heart.

LXIX.

Upon the Weather cock.

BRave, Weather-cock, I fee thou't fet thy Nofe,
  Againft the Wind, which way fo 'ere it blows:
So let a Chriftian in any wife,
Face it with Antichrift in each difguize.

LXX.

Upon a Sheet of white Paper:

THis fubject is unto the fouleft Pen,
  Or faireft, handled by the Sons of Men.
Twill alfo fhew what is upon it writ,
Be t wifely, or non-fence, for want of wit.
Each blot, and blur, it alfo will expofe,
To thy next Readers, be they Friends, or Foes.

Comparifon,

Comparison.

Some Souls are like unto this Blank or Sheet,
(Tho not in Whiteness:) the next man they meet;
If wise, or Fool, debauched, or Deluder,
Or what you will, the dangerous Intruder
May write thereon, to cause that man to err,
In Doctrine, or in Life, with blot and blur.
    Nor will that Soul conceal from who observes,
But shew how foul it is, wherein it swerves:
A reading man may know who was the Writer,
And by the Hellish Non-sence, the Inditer.

LXXI.

Upon the Boy dull at his Book.

SOme Boys have Wit enough to sport and play,
    Who at their Books are Block-heads day by day.
Some men are arch enough at any Vice,
But Dunces in the way to Paradice,

LXXII.

Upon Time and Eternity.

ETernity is like unto a Ring.
    Time, like to Measure, doth it self extend;

Meafure commences, is a finite thing.
The Ring has no beginning, middle, end.

LXXIII.

Upon Fire.

WHo falls into the Fire fhall burn with heat ;
    While thofe remote fcorn from it to retreat.
Yea while thofe in it, cry out, oh *!* I burn.
Some farther off thofe crys to Laughter turn.

Comparifon.

While fome tormented are in Hell for fin ;
On Earth fome greatly do delight therein.
Yea while fome make it eccho with their Cry,
Others count it a Fable and a Lye.

LXXIV.

Of Beauty.

BEauty, at beft is but as fading Flow'rs,
    Bright now, anon with darkfome Clouds it low'rs.
'Tis but skin-deep, and therefore muft decay;
Times blowing on it fends it quite away.
    Then why fhould it be, as it is, admired,
By one and to'ther, and fo much defired.
Things flitting we fhould moderately ufe,
Or we by them our felves fhall much abufe.

THE

THE

CONTENTS

F I N I S

(?)